"I should probably bring another bucket of water, right?"

"Just to be sure. I'm sorry I can't help you."

"You're helping, believe me." She gave her sleeping child a tender glance before taking the bucket back over to the outside spigot.

Finn felt the weight of the five-year-old boy against him as if it were lead. Pressing him down into the lawn chair.

Pressing him into his past.

He'd held his own son just like this. It was such a sweet age, still small enough to fit into a lap and to want to be there.

Leo would soon grow beyond such tenderness.

Derek wouldn't, not ever.

The knowledge of that ached in Finn's chest. Outside of the guilt and the regret, he just plain missed his son.

Kayla sloshed another bucket over the fire pit. "There. No sparks left to cause a fire."

He met her eyes and the thought flashed through him: *There are still some sparks here, just not the fire-pit kind.*

But although it was true, it wouldn't do to highlight the fact.

Lee Tobin McClain read *Gone with the Wind* in the third grade and has been a hopeless romantic ever since. When she's not writing angst-filled love stories with happy endings, she's getting inspiration from her church singles group, her gymnastics-obsessed teenage daughter, and her rescue dog and cat. In her day job, Lee gets to encourage aspiring romance writers in Seton Hill University's low-residency MFA program. Visit her at leetobinmcclain.com.

Books by Lee Tobin McClain

Love Inspired

Redemption Ranch

The Soldier's Redemption

Rescue River

Engaged to the Single Mom
His Secret Child
Small-Town Nanny
The Soldier and the Single Mom
The Soldier's Secret Child
A Family for Easter

Christmas Twins

Secret Christmas Twins

Lone Star Cowboy League: Boys Ranch

The Nanny's Texas Christmas

The Soldier's Redemption

Lee Tobin McClain

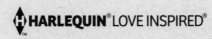

Recycling programs
for this product may
not exist in your area.

LOVE INSPIRED BOOKS

ISBN-13: 978-1-335-50960-4

The Soldier's Redemption

Copyright © 2018 by Lee Tobin McClain

www.Harlequin.com

Printed in U.S.A.

And the people, when they knew it,
followed him: and he received them,
and spake unto them of the kingdom of God,
and healed them that had need of healing.
—*Luke* 9:11

To the staff and volunteers at Animal Friends of Westmoreland. Thank you for letting me work alongside you to learn how a dog rescue operates…and thank you for being a voice for those who cannot speak for themselves.

Chapter One

Finn Gallagher leaned his cane against the desk and swiveled his chair around to face the open window. He loved solitude, but with overseeing Redemption Ranch's kennels, dealing with suppliers and workers and the public, he didn't get enough of it. These early-morning moments when he could sip coffee and look out across the flat plain toward the Sangre de Cristo Mountains were precious and few.

He was reaching over to turn on the window fan—June in Colorado could be hot—when he heard a knock behind him. "Pardon me," said a quiet female voice. "I've come about the job."

So much for solitude.

He swiveled around and got the impression of a small brown sparrow. Plain, with no identifying markers. Brown tied-back hair, gray flannel shirt, jeans, no-brand sneakers.

Well, she was plain until you noticed those high cheekbones and striking blue eyes.

"How'd you find us?" he asked.

"Ad in the paper." She said it Southern style: "Aaa-yud." Not from around here. "Kennel assistant, general cleaning."

"Come on in. Sit down," he said and gestured to a chair, not because he wanted her there but because he felt rude sitting while she was standing. And his days of getting to his feet the moment a lady walked into the room were over. "I'm Finn Gallagher. I run the day-to-day operations here at the ranch."

"Kayla White." She sat down like a sparrow, too, perching. Ready for flight.

"Actually," he said, "for this position, we were looking for a man."

She lifted an eyebrow. "That's discriminatory. I can do the work. I'm stronger than I look."

He studied her a little closer and noticed that she wore long sleeves, buttoned down. In this heat? Weird. She looked healthy, not like a druggie hiding track marks, but lately more and more people seemed to be turning in that desperate direction.

"It's pretty remote here." He'd rather she removed herself from consideration for the job so he wouldn't have to openly turn her down. She was right about the discrimination thing. With all their financial troubles, the last thing Redemption Ranch needed was a lawsuit. "A good ten miles to the nearest town, over bad roads."

She nodded patiently. And didn't ask to be withdrawn from consideration.

"The position requires you to live in. Not much chance to meet people and socialize." He glanced at her bare left hand.

"I'm not big on socializing. More of a bookworm, actually."

That almost made him like her. He spent most of his evenings at home with a dog and a good book, himself. "Small cabin," he warned.

"I'll fit." She gestured at her petite self as the hint of a smile crossed her face and was just as quickly gone. "I'm relocating," she clarified, "so living in would be easier than finding a job and a place to stay, both."

So she wasn't going to give up. Which was fine, really; there was no reason the new hire had to be male. He just had a vision of a woman needing a lot of attention and guidance, gossiping up a blue streak, causing trouble with the veterans.

Both his mother and his boss would have scolded him for that type of prejudice.

Anyway, Kayla seemed independent and not much of a talker. The more Finn looked at her, though, the more he thought she might cause a little interest, at least, among the guys.

And if she were using... "There's a drug test," he said abruptly and watched her reaction.

"Not a problem." Her response was instant and unambiguous.

Okay, then. Maybe she was a possibility.

They talked through the duties of the job—feeding and walking the dogs, some housekeeping in the offices, but mostly cleaning kennels. She had experience cleaning, references. She liked dogs. She'd done cooking, too, which wasn't a need had now, but they might in the future.

Now he wasn't sure if he wanted to talk her into the job or talk her out of it. Something about her, some hint of self-sufficiency, made him like her, at least as much as he liked any woman. And they did need to hire someone soon. But he got the feeling there was a lot she wasn't saying.

Would it be okay to have a woman around? He tested

the notion on himself. He didn't date, didn't deserve to after what he'd done. That meant he spent almost no time around women his age. A nice, quiet woman might be a welcome change.

Or she might be a big complication he didn't need.

"What's the living situation?" she asked. "You said a cabin. Where's it located?"

He gestured west. "There's a row of seven cabins. Small, like I said. And a little run-down. Seeing as you're female, we'd put you on the end of the row—that's what we did with the one female vet who stayed here—but eventually they'll fill up, mostly with men. Veterans with issues."

She blanched, visibly.

He waited. From the bird feeder outside his window, a chickadee scolded. The smell of mountain sage drifted in.

"What kind of issues?" Her voice came out a little husky.

"PTSD related, mostly. Some physical disabilities, too. Anything that would cause a vet to give up hope, is how the owner of the ranch puts it. We give residents a place to get their heads together, do some physical labor and help some four-legged critters who need it. The idea is to help them get back on their feet."

She looked away, out the window, chewing on her lower lip.

He took pity. "We don't allow any firearms. No drugs or alcohol. And we have a couple of mental health specialists and a doctor on call. Planning on a chaplain, too." *Once we start bringing in enough money to hire one*, he almost added, but didn't. "If somebody's problems seem too much for us to handle, we refer them elsewhere."

"I see." She looked thoughtful.

They should've put what kind of nonprofit it was in the ad, to screen out people who were scared of veterans. But the truth was, they'd limited the ad to the fewest words possible, economizing.

"I can show you around," he said. "If you like what you see, we can talk more."

He was pretty sure that conversation wouldn't happen, judging by the way her attitude had changed once their focus on veterans had come up.

He hoisted himself to his feet, grabbed his cane and started toward the door.

She'd stood up to follow, but when she saw him full-length, she took a step back.

It shouldn't surprise him. Even with the inch or so he'd lost from the spinal surgery, he was still six-four. And he'd been lifting to work off some steam. Pretty much The Incredible Hulk.

It had used to work in his favor with women, at least some of them, way back when that had mattered.

"You're military?" she asked as he gestured for her to walk out ahead of him.

"Yep." He waited for the fake *thank you for your service*.

She didn't say it. "What branch?" she asked.

He was closing the door behind them. When he turned to answer, he saw that she'd moved ahead and was kneeling down in front of a little boy who sat on the floor of the outer office, his back against the wall, holding a small gaming device.

Finn sucked in a breath, restrained a surprised exclamation, tried to compose himself.

Kid looked to be about five. Freckle faced and towheaded.

Just like Derek.

His emotions churning, he watched her tap the boy's chin to get his attention. Odd that such a small boy had been so quiet during the, what, half hour that they'd been talking. Derek could never have done it.

"My son, Leo," she said, glancing up at Finn. And then, to the boy: "We're going to walk around with Mr. Gallagher. We might have a place to stay for a bit, a tiny little house."

The boy's eyes lit up and he opened his mouth to speak. Then he looked over at Finn and snapped it shut. He scooted farther behind his mother.

Could the kid be afraid of his limp or his cane? Could Kayla? But if she couldn't deal with that, or her kid couldn't, then they needed to take themselves far away from Redemption Ranch. His problems were minor compared to some of the veterans who would soon be staying here.

And beyond that, what kind of risks would a young kid face in a place like this? The vets he wasn't really worried about, but a little kid could be trouble around dogs—if he was too afraid of them, or not afraid enough.

No kids were going to be hurt on Finn's watch. Never again.

"This way," he said, his voice brusque. He'd show them around, because he had said he would. Unlike a lot of people, he didn't retract his promises.

He touched her back to guide her out. As he felt the

ridge of her spine through the shirt, she looked up at him, eyes wide and startled.

He withdrew his hand immediately, his face heating. He hadn't meant his touch to be flirtatious, but apparently it had come off some weird way.

He could already tell this wasn't going to work.

Kayla pulled Leo close beside her as she walked ahead of the square-shouldered soldier into the open air. Her mind raced at strategic pace.

She'd gotten a good feeling about the job when she'd seen it, reading the *Esperanza Springs Mountaineer* in the café where they'd had an early breakfast. Live in— check. They needed a place to live. A good thousand miles away from Arkansas, remote and off the beaten path—check. That was the big priority. Work she could handle—check. She liked dogs, and she liked working hands-on.

A wholesome, healthy, happy environment that would help Leo heal… Of that, she wasn't yet sure.

As for her own healing from her terrible marriage, she wasn't expecting that, and it didn't matter. She wasn't the type to elicit love from anyone, her son the exception. She knew that for sure, now.

The man striding beside her—and how did a guy stride with a cane, anyway?—looked a little too much like her bodybuilding, short-haired, military-postured ex. Finn had spooked her son to the point where, now, Leo pressed close into her side, making it hard to walk.

But it wasn't like she was going to become best friends with this Finn Gallagher, if she did get this job and decide to take it. It wasn't like she'd reveal anything to him, to anyone, that could somehow lead to Mitch finding them.

The mountains rose in a semicircle around the flat basin where the ranch was situated, white streaks of snow decorating the peaks even at the end of June. There was a weathered-looking barn up ahead of them, and off to the right, a pond with a dock and a rowboat.

This place drew her in. It was beautiful, and about as far from Little Rock as they could reasonably go, given the car she was driving. If she were just basing things on geography, she'd snap this job up in a minute.

But the military angle worried her.

"Would we live there?" Leo pointed. His voice was quiet, almost a whisper, but in it she detected a trace of excitement.

They were approaching a small log cabin with a couple of rustic chairs on a narrow porch. As Finn had mentioned, it was the end of a row of similar structures. Sunlight glinted off its green tin roof. One of the shutters hung crooked, but other than that, the place looked sturdy enough.

"This is the cabin you'd live in if this works out," Finn said, glancing down at Leo and then at her. "The vet who lived here before just moved out, so it should be pretty clean. Come on in."

Inside, the cabin's main room had a kitchen area—sink and refrigerator and stove—along the far wall. A door to one side looked like it led to a bathroom or closet. A simple, rough-hewn dining table, a couch and a couple of chairs filled up the rest of the small room. With some throw rugs and homemade curtains, it would be downright cozy.

"Sleeping loft is upstairs," Finn said, indicating a sturdy, oversize ladder.

Leo's head whipped around to look at Kayla. He loved to climb as much as any little boy.

"Safe up there?" she asked Finn. "Anything that could hurt a kid?" She could already see that the sleeping area had a three-foot railing at the edge, which would prevent a fall.

"It's childproof." His voice was gruff.

"No guns, knives, nothing?" If Finn were like Mitch, he'd be fascinated by weapons. And he wouldn't consider them a danger to a kid.

"Of course not!" Finn looked so shocked and indignant that she believed him.

"Go ahead—climb up and take a look," she said to her son. Leo had been cooped up in the car during the past four days. She wanted to seize any possible opportunity for him to have fun.

She stood at the bottom of the ladder and watched him climb, quick and agile. She heard his happy exclamation, and then his footsteps tapped overhead as he ran from one side of the loft to the other.

Love for him gripped her hard. She'd find a way to make him a better life, whether here or somewhere else.

"I'm not sure this is the right environment for a child," Finn said in a low voice. He was standing close enough that she could smell his aftershave, some old-fashioned scent her favorite stepfather had used. "We need someone who'll work hard, and if you're distracted by a kid, you can't."

"There's a camp program at the church in Esperanza Springs. Thought we'd check that out." Actually, she already had, online; they had daily activities, were open to five-year-olds and offered price breaks to low-income families.

Which they definitely were.

Finn didn't say anything, and silent men made her nervous. "Leo," she called, "come on down."

Her son scrambled down the ladder and pressed into her leg, looking warily at Finn.

Curiosity flared in the big man's eyes, but he didn't ask questions. Instead, he walked over to the door and held it open. "I'll show you the kennels." His face softened as he looked down at Leo. "We have eighteen dogs right now."

Leo didn't speak, but he glanced up at Kayla and gave a little jump. She knew what it meant. Eighteen dogs would be a cornucopia of joy to him.

They headed along the road in front of the cabins. "Is he comfortable with dogs?" Finn asked.

"He hasn't been around them much, but he's liked the ones he's met." Loved, more like. A pet was one of the things she'd begged Mitch for, regularly. She'd wanted the companionship for Leo, because she'd determined soon after his birth that they'd never have another child. Fatherhood didn't sit well with Mitch.

But Mitch hadn't wanted a dog, and she'd known better than to go against him on that. She wouldn't be the only one who'd suffer; the dog would, too, and Leo.

"We're low on residents right now," Finn said. He waved a hand toward a rustic, hotel-like structure half-hidden by the curve of a hill. "Couple of guys live in the old lodge. Help us do repairs, when they have time. But they both work days and aren't around a whole lot."

"You going to fill the place up?"

"Slowly, as we get the physical structures back up to code. These two cabins are unoccupied." He gestured to the two that were next to the one he'd just shown them. The corner of one was caving in, and its porch looked unstable. She'd definitely have to set some limits on where Leo could play, in the event that this worked out. "This next one, guy named Parker lives there, but he's away. His mom's real sick. I'm not sure when he'll be back."

Across the morning air, the sound of banjo and guitar music wafted, surprising her. She looked down at Leo, whose head was cocked to one side.

They found the source of the music on the porch of the last cabin, and as they came close, the men playing the instruments stopped. "Who you got there?" came a raspy voice.

Finn half turned to her. "Come meet Willie and Long John. Willie lives in the cabin next door, but he spends most of his time with Long John. If you work here, you'll see a lot of them."

As they approached the steps, the two men got to their feet. They both looked to be in their later sixties. The tall, skinny, balding one who'd struggled getting up had to be Long John, which meant the short, heavyset one, with a full white beard, his salt-and-pepper hair pulled back in a ponytail, must be Willie. Both wore black Vietnam veteran baseball caps.

Finn introduced them and explained why Kayla was here.

"Hope you'll take the job," Long John said. "We could use some help with the dogs."

"And it'd improve the view around here," Willie said, a smile quirking the corner of his mouth beneath the beard.

Finn cleared his throat and glared at the older man.

Willie just grinned and eased down onto the cabin's

steps. At eye level with Leo, he held out a hand. "I'm pleased to meet you, young man," he said.

"Shake hands," Kayla urged, and Leo held out his right hand.

"Pleased to meet you, sir," he said, his voice almost a whisper, and Kayla felt a surge of pride at his manners.

After a grave handshake, Willie looked up at her. "Wouldn't mind having a little guy around here. Always did like to take my grandkids fishing." He waved an arm in the direction of the pond she'd seen. "We keep it stocked."

Kayla's heart melted, just at the edges. Grandfather figures for Leo? A chance for him to learn to fish?

There was a low *woof* from inside the screen door and a responding one from the porch. A large black dog she hadn't seen before lumbered to its feet.

"About time you noticed there's some new folks here," Long John said, reaching from his chair to run a hand over the black dog's bony spine. "Rockette, here, don't pay a whole lot of attention to the world these days. Not unless her friend Duke wakes her up."

Willie opened the screen door. A gray-muzzled pit bull sauntered out.

"Duke. Sit." Willie made a hand gesture, and Duke obediently dropped to his haunches, his tongue lolling out. Willie slipped a treat from the pocket of his baggy jeans and fed it to the dog.

Leo took two steps closer to the old black dog, reached out and touched its side with the tips of his fingers.

"One of our agreements, for anyone who lives in the cabins, is that they take in a dog," Finn explained. "Gives them a little extra attention. Especially the ones not likely to be adopted."

Leo tugged Kayla's hand. "Would *we* have a dog?"

"Maybe." She put seriousness into her voice so he wouldn't get his hopes up. "It all depends if Mr. Gallagher decides to offer me the job, and if I take it. Those are grown-up decisions."

"Sure could use the help," Long John said, lowering himself back into his chair with a stifled groan. "Me and Willie been doing our best, but…" He waved a hand at a walker folded against the porch railing. "With my Parkinson's, it's not that easy."

"Hardly anyone else has applied," Willie added. "Don't get many out-of-towners around these parts. And the people who live in Esperanza Springs heard we're gonna have more guys up here. They get skittish." He winked at Kayla. "We vets are gentle as lambs, though, once you get to know us."

"Right." She had direct experience to the contrary.

At first, before her marriage had gone so far downhill, she hadn't translated Mitch's problems into a mistrust of all military personnel. Later, it had been impossible to avoid doing just that.

When Mitch had pushed his way into her place well after their divorce was final—talking crazy and roughing her up—she'd gone to the police.

She hadn't wanted to file a complaint, which had been stupid. She'd just wanted to know her options, whether a protection order would do any good.

What she hadn't known was that the police officer she'd spoken with was army, too. Hadn't known he drank with Mitch at the Legion.

The cop had let Mitch know that she'd reported him, and she still bore the bruises from when he'd come back over to her place, enraged, looking for blood.

Shaking off her thoughts, she watched Long John talk with Finn while Willie plucked at his guitar and then held it out to show Leo. The two veterans did exude a gentle vibe. But then, their wartime experiences were distant, their aggressions most likely tamed through age and experience.

"Let's take a look at the kennels," Finn said and nodded toward the barn. "Later, guys."

Just outside the barn, Finn turned and gestured for Leo to stand in front of him. After a nod from Kayla, Leo did, his eyes lowered, shoulders frozen in a slump.

"I want you to ask before you touch a dog, Leo," he said. "Most of them are real nice, but a couple are nervous enough to lash out. So ask an adult first, and never, ever open a kennel without an adult there to help you. Understand?"

Leo nodded, taking a step closer to Kayla.

"Good." Finn turned toward the barn door and beckoned for them to follow him.

Much barking greeted their entry into the dim barn. Finn flicked on a light, revealing kennels along both sides of the old structure and more halfway up the middle. One end of the barn was walled off into what looked like an office.

Finn walked down the row of dogs, telling her their names, reaching through some of the wire fencing to stroke noses. His fondness for the animals was obvious in his tone and his gentle touch. "All of them are seniors," he explained over his shoulder. "Which is about seven and up for a big dog, eight or nine for a little one."

"Where do they come from?" she asked. The barking had died down, and most of the dogs stood at the gates of their kennels, tails wagging, eyes begging for attention.

"Owner surrenders, mostly. Couple of strays."

She knelt to look at a red-gold dog, probably an Irish setter mix. "Why would anyone give you up, sweetie?" She reached between the cage wires to touch the dog's white muzzle, seeming to read sadness in its eyes.

"Lots of reasons," Finn said. "People move. Or they don't have money for food and vet bills. Sometimes, they just don't want to deal with a dog that requires some extra care." He knelt beside her. "Lola, here, she can't make it up and down stairs. Her owner lived in a two-story house, so…"

"They couldn't carry her up and down?"

"Apparently not."

"Can I pet her, too, Mom?" Leo asked, forgetting to be quiet.

Kayla looked over at Finn. "Can he?"

"She's harmless. Go ahead."

As Leo stuck fingers into the cage of the tail-wagging Lola, Finn turned toward Kayla. "Most of our dogs *are* really gentle, just like I was telling Leo. The ones that are reactive have a red star on their cages." He pointed to one on the cage of a medium-sized brown dog, some kind of Doberman mix. "Those, you both stay away from. If the job works out, we'll talk about getting you some training for handling difficult dogs."

If the job worked out. Would it work out? Did she want it to?

Finn had moved farther down the row of cages, and he made a small sound of concern and opened one, guiding a black cocker spaniel out and attaching a leash to her collar. He bent over the little dog, rubbing his hands up and down her sides. "It's okay," he murmured as the dog wagged her tail and leaned against him. "You're okay."

"What's wrong?"

"Her cage is a mess. She knocked over her water and spilled her food." He scratched behind her ears. "Never has an accident, though, do you, girl?"

Kayla felt her shoulders loosen just a fraction. If Finn was that kind and gentle with a little dog, maybe he was a safe person to be around.

"Could you hold her leash while I clean up her cage?" he asked, looking over at Kayla. "In fact, if you wouldn't mind, she needs to go outside."

"No problem." She moved to take the leash and knelt down, Leo hurrying to her side.

"Careful," Finn warned. "She's blind and mostly deaf. You have to guide her or she'll run into things."

"How can she walk?" Leo asked, squatting down beside Kayla and petting the dog's back as Finn had done. "Mom, feel her! She's soft!"

Kayla put her hand in the dog's fur, shiny and luxuriant. "She *is* soft."

"She still has a good sense of smell," Finn explained to Leo. "And the sun and grass feel good to her. You'll see." He gestured toward the door at the opposite end of the barn. "There's a nice meadow out there where the dogs can run."

She and Leo walked toward the barn's door, guiding the dog around an ancient tractor and bins of dog food. In the bright meadow outside, Kayla inhaled the sweet, pungent scents of pine and wildflowers.

"Look, Mom, she's on her back!" Leo said. "She likes it out here!"

Kayla nodded, kneeling beside Leo to watch the little black dog's ecstatic rolling and arching. "She sure does. No matter that she has some problems—nobody likes to be in a cage."

A few minutes later, Finn came out, leading another dog. "I see you've figured out her favorite activity," he said. "Thanks for helping."

The dog he was leading, some kind of a beagle-basset mix, nudged the blind dog, and they sniffed each other. Then the hound jumped up and bumped her to the ground.

"He's hurting her!" Leo cried and stepped toward the pair.

"Let them be." Finn's hands came down on Leo's shoulders, gently stopping him.

Leo edged away and stood close to Kayla.

Finn lifted an eyebrow and then smiled reassuringly at Leo. "She's a real friendly dog and likes to play. Wish I could find someone to adopt her, but with her disabilities, it's hard. Willie and Long John can only handle one dog each. I have one of our problem dogs at my place—" He waved off toward a small house next to a bigger one, in the direction of the lodge. "And Penny— she owns the ranch—has another at hers. So for now, this girl stays in the kennel."

If she and Leo stayed here, maybe they could take the black dog in. That would certainly make Leo happy. He'd sunk down to roll on the ground with the dogs, laughing as they licked his face, acting like a puppy himself. He hadn't smiled so much in weeks.

And Kayla, who always weighed her choices carefully, who'd spent a year planning how to divorce Mitch, made a snap decision.

This place was safe. It was remote. Mitch would never find them. And maybe Leo could have a decent childhood for a while. Not forever, she didn't expect that, but a little bit of a safe haven.

She looked over at Finn. He was smiling, too, watching Leo. It softened his hard-planed, square face, made him almost handsome. But as he watched, his mouth twisted a little, and his sea-blue eyes got distant.

She didn't want him to sink into a bad mood. That was never good. "If I can arrange for the summer camp for Leo," she said, "I'd be very interested in the job."

He looked at her, then at Leo, and then at the distant mountains. "There's paperwork, a reference check, drug tests. All that would have to be taken care of before we could offer you anything permanent."

"Not a problem." Not only did she have good references, but they were sworn to secrecy as to her whereabouts.

"I'll have to talk to our owner, too." His voice held reluctance.

Time to be blunt. "Is there some kind of problem you see in hiring me?"

"I'm withholding judgment," he said. "But we *do* need someone soon, since our last assistant quit. Until everything's finalized, how about a one-week trial?"

"That works." Even if the job didn't come together, she and Leo would get a week off the road.

With dogs.

Meanwhile, Finn's extreme caution made her curious. "You never did mention what branch of the military you served in," she said as he bent over to put leashes back on the two tired-out dogs.

"Eighty-second Airborne."

Kayla sat down abruptly beside Leo, pulling her knees to herself on the grassy ground. She knew God was good and had a plan, but sometimes it seemed like He was toying with her.

Because this perfect new job meant involvement with a man from the same small, intensely loyal division of the US Army as her abusive ex.

Chapter Two

"You sure you're not making a big mistake?" Penny Jordan asked Finn two days later.

It was Saturday afternoon, and they were sitting in Penny's office, watching out the window as Kayla's subcompact sputtered up the dirt road to cabin six, leaving a trail of black exhaust in its wake.

"No." Finn watched as Kayla exited the car and opened the back door. Leo climbed out, and they opened the hatch and stood, surveying its contents. Leo looked up at her, listening seriously, like an adult. "I think it probably *is* a mistake, but I couldn't talk her out of wanting the job. So I went with the one-week trial."

"But she's moving in." Penny, ten years older than Finn but at least twenty times wiser, took a gulp of black coffee from her oversize cup. "That doesn't seem like a trial thing to do."

"They were staying at the campground up toward Harmony." He eased his leg off the chair where he'd been resting it, grimacing. "Afternoon thunderstorms are getting bad. At least they'll have a roof over their heads."

"You're skirting the issue." Penny leaned forward, elbows on the table. "She has a young son."

"I know, and even though she says she's got a plan for childcare, I don't know that it's safe for him—"

"Finn." Penny put a hand on his arm. "You know what I'm talking about."

He wasn't going there. "Guess I'd better get up there and help 'em move in."

"You're going to have to face what happened one of these days," she said, standing up with her trademark speed and grace. "I'll come, too. Gotta meet the woman who broke through your three-foot-thick walls."

"She didn't break through—it's a *trial*," he emphasized. "She knows the deal. And yes, you should meet her, because when she's not working kennels she can do housekeeping for you. Free you up for the real work."

Penny put her hands on her hips and arched forward and sideways, stretching her back. She was slim, with one long braid down her back and fine wrinkles fanning out from the corners of her eyes, the result of years spent outdoors in the Western sun. Not a trace of makeup, but she didn't need it; she was naturally pretty. Big heart, too.

She didn't deserve what had happened to her.

"Speaking of the real work," she said, "we might have two more vets coming in within the next six weeks."

"Oh?"

"Guy's classic PTSD, right out of Iraq. The woman…" Penny shook her head. "She's been through it. Scarred up almost as bad as Daniela was." Penny walked over to the window and looked out, her forehead wrinkling. "I'm going to put her in the cabin next to your new hire. She'll be more comfortable farther away from the guys."

Finn nodded. Daniela Jiminez had only recently left the ranch to marry another short-term resident, Gabriel Shafer. They'd stopped in to visit after their honeymoon, and their obvious joy mostly made Finn happy. He'd never experience that for himself, didn't deserve to, but he was glad to have had a small part in getting Gabe and Daniela together.

They walked down the sunny lane to the cabins. Finn kept up with Penny's quick stride even though he wasn't using his cane; it was a good day.

When they were halfway down, Willie's truck came toward them and glided to a halt. "Hitting the roadhouse for dinner and then a little boot scootin'," Willie said out the window. "You should come along, Finn. Meet somebody."

Penny rolled her eyes. "Men."

"Like Finn's gonna get a lady friend," Long John said from the passenger seat.

"You think you've got better odds?" Finn asked, meaning it as a joke. Everyone knew he didn't go out, didn't date. Those who pushed had gotten their heads bitten off and learned a lesson. Willie and Long John, though, were more persistent than most.

"We've both got better odds because we know how to smile and socialize," Willie said. "Ladies around here love us."

That was probably true. Unlike Finn, they both had the capacity for connection, the ability to form good relationships. He, on the other hand, didn't have the personality that meshed easily with a woman's. Too quiet, too serious. Deirdre had thrown that fact at him every time he caught her cheating.

"Y'all be careful, now," Penny said, giving the two

men a stern look. "You know we don't hold with drinking at the ranch, and that roadhouse is the eye of the storm."

"Rum and coke, hold the rum," Willie promised.

"Scout's honor," Long John said, holding up a hand in mock salute.

The truck pulled away, and a couple of minutes later Finn and Penny reached the cabin driveway where Kayla was unloading her car. She put down her box, picked up a red rubber ball and squatted in front of her son. "You say hello," she told the boy, "and then you can go throw the ball against the house."

The little boy swallowed, and his eyes darted in their direction and away. "Hi," he said and then grabbed the ball and ran to the side of the cabin.

"He's a little shy," Kayla said. She extended a hand to Penny. "I'm Kayla White. Are you Penny?"

"That's right." Penny gave Kayla a frank appraisal. "I'm glad to meet you. Looking forward to having a little help around here. See how you like the work. And how the work likes you. Cleaning up after dogs isn't for everyone."

"I've done worse." Kayla's color rose, like she'd read a challenge under Penny's words. "I appreciate the chance to stay in the cabin, but we're not going to really settle in until the trial week's over. I know the job wasn't intended for a mother and child."

"Sometimes the Good Lord surprises us," Penny said. "Now, what can we do to help you move in?"

"Not a thing." Kayla brushed her hands on the sides of her jeans. "I'm about done. And I can do some work tomorrow, although it'll be limited by Leo. I'm going to have him try that church camp on Monday." She shaded her eyes to watch her son as he threw the ball against the house, caught it and threw it again.

Looking at young Leo, Finn felt the lid on his memories start to come loose. Derek had loved to play ball, too. Finn had spent a lot of time teaching him to throw and catch and use a bat. Things a father was supposed to teach his son.

His throat tightened, and he coughed to clear it. "We'll take care of the work your first day here. You can start on Monday." He was feeling the urge to be away from her and her child.

She looked from Finn to Penny. "Well, but you're giving me a place to stay early. I don't want to be beholden." She pushed back a strand of chocolate hair that had escaped her ponytail and fallen into her eyes.

She was compact, but strong, with looks that grew on you slowly. Good thing she wasn't his type. Back when he was in the market for a woman, he'd gone for bigger, bouncier, louder ladies. The fun kind.

Yeah, and look where that got you.

"I'm with Finn on having you start Monday, but I'll tell you what," Penny said. "We all go down to church on Sundays. Why don't you join us? It'll give your son a chance to get to know some of the other kids while you're still nearby. That should make his first day at camp a little easier."

Finn turned his face so Kayla couldn't see it and glared at Penny. Yeah, he'd hired Kayla—temporarily—but that didn't mean they had to get all chummy in their time off.

Still, it was church. He supposed he ought to be more welcoming. And he knew Penny missed her grown daughter, who for inexplicable reasons had sided with her father when Penny's marriage had broken up. If Penny wanted to mother Kayla a little, he shouldn't get in the way.

Kayla bit her lip. "I'd like to get Leo to church," she said. "We went some back home, but…well. It wasn't as often as I'd have liked. I want to change that, now."

So she'd be coming to church with them every Sunday if she took the job? It wasn't as if there was much of a choice; Esperanza Springs had only two churches, so it was fifty-fifty odds she'd choose theirs.

Unless she wanted to get some breathing room, too.

Or maybe she'd leave after a week. He intended to make sure the work was hard and long, so that she didn't get too comfortable here.

Because something about Kayla White was making *him* feel anything but comfortable.

As the church service ended in a burst of uplifting piano music, Kayla leaned back in the pew. Her whole body felt relaxed for the first time in weeks. Months, really.

The little church had plain padded benches and a rough-hewn altar. Outside the clear glass windows, the splendor of the mountains put to shame any human effort at stained glass artistry.

Leo had sat with her for half the service, reluctantly gone up to the children's sermon and then followed the other kids out of the sanctuary with a desperate look back at Kayla. She'd forced herself not to rescue him and had made it ten minutes before giving in to her worries and going to check on him. She'd found him busily making crafts with the other young children, looking, if not happy, at least focused.

Now beside her Penny stretched, stood and then sat back down. "Hey, I forgot to mention that Finn and I help serve lunch after church to the congregation and some hard-up folks in the community. Would you like to join us? If you don't feel like working, you can just mingle until lunch is served."

The pastor—young, tanned and exuberant—had been visiting with the few people remaining in the pews, and he reached them just as Penny finished speaking. "We find we get more people to come to church when we offer a free meal," he said and held out a hand to Kayla. "Welcome. We're glad to have you here. I'm Carson Blair."

"Kayla White. I enjoyed your sermon."

He was opening his mouth to reply when two little girls, who looked to be a bit older than Leo, ran down the aisle at breakneck speed. They flung themselves at the pastor, one clinging to each leg, identical pouts on their faces.

"Daddy, she hit me!"

"She started it!"

The pastor knelt down. "Skye, you need to go sit right there." He indicated a pew on the left-hand side. "And, Sunny, you sit over here." He pointed to the right.

"But…"

"We wanted to play!" The one he'd called Sunny looked mournfully at her twin.

"Sit quietly for five minutes, and you can play together again."

Kayla smiled as the pastor turned back toward the small circle of adults. "Good tactics," she said. "I have a five-year-old. I can't imagine handling two."

Finn pushed himself out of the pew and ended up standing next to Kayla, leaning on his cane, facing the pastor. "Had a phone message from you," he said to the pastor. "I'm sorry I didn't return it. Weekend got away from me."

"We all know your aversion to the phone," the pastor said, reaching out to shake Finn's extended hand.

"To conversation in general," Penny said. "Finn's the strong, silent type," she added to Kayla.

"Don't listen to them," Finn advised and then turned back toward the pastor. "What's up?"

"I was hoping to talk to you about your chaplain position. I know you can't pay yet, but I'd be glad to conduct vespers once a week, or do a little counseling, as long as it doesn't take away from my work here."

"I'll keep that in mind."

Finn's answer didn't seem very gracious for someone who'd just been offered volunteer services.

The pastor looked at him steadily. "Do that."

"We certainly will," Penny said. "But speaking of work, that lunch won't get served without us. You coming?" she asked Kayla.

"Absolutely. Lunch smells wonderful. I'm happy to help, if it will get me a plate of whatever's cooking."

"We all partake," the pastor said, shaking her hand again vigorously. "We're glad to have you here. It's rare that we get a fresh face."

"Won't be so rare soon," Penny warned. "We have a couple of new veterans coming in. And I'm working on getting Long John and Willie to church, too."

"You know the church does a van run," the pastor

said. "Sounds like you'll need it. And we'll gladly welcome the men and women who served our country."

Finn jerked his head to the side. "Let's go."

In the church kitchen, organized chaos reigned. Finn handed aprons to Kayla and Penny and then donned one himself, choosing it from a special hook labeled with his name.

"Why do you get your own apron?" she asked, because there didn't seem to be anything special about it.

"It's king-size," he said ruefully. "Those little things barely cover a quarter of me. Last Christmas, the volunteers went together to buy me this tent."

"And in return," a white-haired woman said, "we make him carry all the heavy trays and boxes. Isn't that right, Finn?"

"Glad to, as long as you save me a piece of your strawberry-rhubarb pie, Mrs. Barnes."

Kayla was put to work dishing up little bowls of fruit salad while Penny helped Mrs. Barnes get everyone seated and Finn pulled steaming trays of chicken and rice from the ovens. A couple of other ladies carried baskets of rolls to each table and mingled with the guests, probably fifty or sixty people in all.

It wasn't a fancy church. As many of the congregation members wore jeans as dresses and suits, and seating for the meal was open. That meant there was no distinction between those who'd come just for the food and those who'd come for the service first. Nice.

The children burst into the room and took over one corner, stocked with toys and a big rug. Kayla waited a minute and then went to check on Leo. She found

him banging action figures with another kid in a zeal-
ous pretend fight.

"Hey, buddy," she said quietly, touching his shoulder.

He flinched and turned. She hated that he did that.
No matter what, she was going to make sure he gained
confidence and stopped feeling like he was at risk all
the time. Mitch had never hit him, to her knowledge,
but yelling and belittling were almost as bad. And
that last time, when he'd broken into their place and
beaten Kayla, she'd looked up from the floor to see Leo
crouched in the doorway, pale and silent, tears running
down his cheeks.

"Leo is quiet, but he seems to fit in," said the woman
who'd run the children's program. "He's a very polite little boy. I understand he's going to do the day camp, too?"

Kayla nodded. "Thank you for taking care of him."

"He's welcome to sit at the kids' table and eat. Most
of the children do, though a few go sit with their parents."

Kayla turned back to Leo. "What do you think,
buddy? Want to sit here with your new friends, or come
sit with me and Miss Penny and Mr. Finn?"

Leo considered.

The other boy whacked his action figure. "ATTACK!"
he yelled.

Leo made his figure strike back, and the other boy
fell on the floor, pretending he'd been struck.

"I'll stay with the kids," Leo said and dived down to
the floor to make his action figure engage in some hand-
to-hand combat with the one the other boy was holding.

Kayla watched them play for a moment as realization struck her. If she did, indeed, build a better life for

Leo, it would mean he'd become more and more independent. He wouldn't be tied to her by fear. He'd have regular friendships, sleepovers at other boys' homes, camping trips.

And where did that leave her, who'd centered her life around protecting her son for the past five years?

It'll leave me right where I should be, she told herself firmly. It would be good, normal, for Leo to gain independence. And if that made her nostalgic for his baby years of total reliance on her, that was normal, too. She could focus on the healthy ways parents and children related, instead of walking on eggshells to avoid offending Mitch.

The lunch went quickly, partly because the serving staff ate in shifts and then hurried back to the kitchen to help with refills and cleanup. Kayla didn't mind. She liked the camaraderie of working with others. And she liked having her stomach—and her son's—full of delicious, healthy food.

She was washing dishes when Mrs. Barnes came up beside her, towel in hand. "I'll dry and put away," she said. "Where are you from, dear?"

"Arkansas," Kayla said vaguely. "Small town." Mrs. Barnes seemed harmless, but Kayla didn't want to get into the habit of revealing too much.

"And what brought you to Esperanza Springs? We don't get a whole lot of newcomers."

Kayla was conscious of Finn nearby, carrying big empty serving dishes back to the sinks to be washed. "I was looking for a change," she said. "I've always loved the mountains, so we thought we'd take our chances in Colorado."

"And what did you do back in Arkansas?"

Kayla didn't see malice in the other woman's eyes, only a little too much curiosity. "I worked for a cleaning company," she said. "Cleaning houses and offices and such." No need to mention that she'd started it, and that it had been doing well. She hoped Janice, who'd taken it over, was managing okay. She'd been avoiding calling her, afraid word would get back to Mitch, but she needed to stop being afraid. She'd call Janice tonight.

The kitchen was getting hotter, and Kayla dried off her hands and unbuttoned her sleeves. As she rolled them up, Mrs. Barnes went still. Behind her, Finn stared, too.

Too late, she looked down and saw her arms, still a traffic wreck of bruises.

"Oh, my, dear, what happened?" Mrs. Barnes put a gentle hand on Kayla's shoulder.

She didn't look at either of them. "I fell."

It wasn't a lie. Each time Mitch had hit her, she'd fallen.

Someone called Mrs. Barnes to the serving counter. She squeezed Kayla's shoulder and then turned away, leaving Finn and Kayla standing at the sink.

He frowned at her, putting his hands on his hips. "If someone hurt you—"

An Eighty-second Airborne tattoo peeked out from under the sleeve of his shirt. The same tattoo Mitch had.

She took a step backward. "I need to go check on Leo," she said abruptly and practically ran out of the kitchen, rolling down her sleeves as she went.

Leo was drawing pictures with the same boy he'd been playing with before, but he jumped up and hugged her when she approached. "Mom! Hector goes to the day camp here, too! He's gonna get me the cubby next to his and bring his Skytrooper tomorrow!" He flopped back down on the floor, propped on his arms, drawing on the same large piece of paper as his new friend.

"That's great, honey." Kayla backed away and looked from Leo to the kitchen and back again. She was well and truly caught.

Her whole goal was to provide a safe, happy home for Leo. And it looked like maybe she'd found that place. The ranch, the dogs, the church people, all were bringing out her son's relaxed, happy side—a side she'd almost forgotten he had.

But on the other hand, there was Finn—a dangerous man by virtue of his association with Mitch's favorite, dedicated social circle. She knew how the Eighty-second worked.

She grabbed a sponge and started wiping down tables, thinking.

Finn had seen her bruises and gotten suspicious. If she let slip too much information, he might just get in touch with Mitch.

On the other hand, maybe his tattoo was old and so was his allegiance. Maybe he'd gotten involved in broader veterans affairs. Not everyone stayed focused on their own little division of the service.

She had to find out more about Finn and how committed he was to his paratrooper brothers. And she had to do it quickly. Because Leo was already starting to get attached to this place, and truthfully, so was she.

But she couldn't let down her guard. She had to learn more.

As she wiped a table, hypnotically, over and over, she concocted a plan. Once she'd finalized it, she felt better.

By this evening, one way or another, she'd have the answer about whether or not they could stay. For Leo's sake, she hoped the answer was yes.

Chapter Three

Late Sunday afternoon, Finn settled into his recliner and put his legs up. He clicked on a baseball game and tried to stop thinking.

It didn't work.

He kept going back to those bruises on Kayla's arms, the defensive secrecy in her eyes. All of it pretty much advertised a victim of abuse.

If that were the case, he was in trouble. His primary responsibility was to the veterans here, and some angry guy coming in to drag Kayla away would up the potential for violence among a group of men who'd seen too much of it.

That was bad.

But worse, he was starting to feel responsible for Kayla and the boy. They were plucky but basically defenseless. They needed protection.

If he sent them away, he'd be putting them at risk.

His phone buzzed, a welcome break from his worries. He clicked to answer. "Gallagher."

"Somethin' curious just happened." It was Long John's voice.

Finn settled back into his chair. "What's that, buddy?" Unlike Willie, Long John had no family, and with his Agent Orange–induced Parkinson's, he couldn't get out a lot. He tended to call Finn with reports of a herd of elk, or an upcoming storm, or a recommendation about caring for one of the dogs.

It was fine, good, even. Finn didn't have much family himself, none here in Colorado, and providing a listening ear to lonely vets gave him a sense of purpose.

Long John cleared his throat. "That Kayla is mighty interested in you."

"What do you mean?" For just a second, he thought Long John meant romantic interest, but then he realized that wasn't likely to be the case. Kayla was young, pretty and preoccupied with her own problems. She wouldn't want to hook up with someone like him. Long John was probably just creating drama out of boredom.

"She came over for a little chat," Long John said. "Talked about the weather a bit and then got right into questions about you."

"What kind of questions?"

"Where'd you serve. How active are you in the local chapter. How many of your military buddies come around. Did you ever do anything with the Eighty-second on the national level. That kind of stuff."

"Weird." Especially since she'd seemed to have an aversion to all things military.

"Not sure what to make of it," Long John said. "She's a real nice gal, but still. All kinds of people trying to take advantage. Thought you should know."

"Thanks." He chatted to the older man for a few more minutes and then ended the call.

Restless now, he strode out onto his porch. The plot

thickened around Kayla. If she'd been treated badly by someone, why would she now be seeking information about Finn? Was she still attached to her abuser? Was he making her gather information for some reason?

As he sat down on the porch steps to rub his leg— today was a bad day—he saw Kayla sitting with Penny at the picnic table beside Penny's house. Talking intently.

More information gathering?

Leo played nearby, some engrossing five-year-old game involving rocks and a lot of shouting. Kid needed a playmate. They should invite the pastor's little girls up here.

Except thinking of the widowed pastor hanging around Kayla rubbed him the wrong way.

And why should any of that matter to him? Impatient with himself, he got down on the ground and started pulling up the weeds that were getting out of control around the foundation of his place, like everywhere else on the ranch. Kayla wasn't his concern. She was here on a temporary pass. And even if they did give her the full-time job—which he still questioned—he didn't need to get involved in how she ran her life and raised her kid.

Penny stood and waved to him. "I'll be inside, doing some paperwork, if anybody needs me," she called.

He stood, gave her a thumbs-up and watched her walk inside. That was how they ran the place, spelling each other, letting each other know what they were doing. It'd be quiet on a Sunday, but they liked for at least one of them to be on call, phone on, ready to help as needed.

From the garden area just behind him, he heard a thump, a wail—"Mommy!"—and then the sound of crying. Leo. Finn spun and went to the boy, who was kneeling on the ground where Finn had been digging. His hand was bleeding and his face wet with tears.

Finn beckoned to Kayla, who'd jumped up from the picnic table, and then knelt awkwardly beside the little boy. "Hey, son, what happened?"

Leo cringed away, his eyebrows drawing together, and cried harder.

"Leo!" Kayla arrived, sank down and drew Leo into her arms. "Oh, no, honey, what happened?"

"It hurts!" Leo clutched his bloody hand to his chest.

"Let me see."

The little boy held up his hand to show her, but the sight of it made him wail louder. "I'm bleeding!"

Kayla leaned in and examined the wound, and Finn did, too. Fortunately, it didn't look too serious. The bleeding was already stopping. "Looks like he might have cut it on the weed digger. Is that what happened, buddy?"

The boy nodded, still gulping and gasping.

"I have bandages and antibiotic cream inside, if you want to bring him in." He knew better than to offer to carry the boy. Only a mother would do at a time like this.

Kayla got to her feet and swung Leo up into her arms. "Come on. Let's fix you up."

There was a buzzing sound, and Finn felt for his phone.

"It's mine," Kayla said. "I'll get it later."

"You can sit in there." Finn indicated the kitchen. "I'll grab the stuff."

Moments later, he was back downstairs with every size of Band-Aid in his cupboard and three different types of medical ointment.

Kayla had Leo sitting on the edge of the sink and was rinsing his hand.

Leo howled like he was being tortured.

"I know, honey, it hurts, but we have to clean it. There. Now it'll start feeling better." She wrapped a paper towel around the boy's hand and lifted him easily from the sink to a kitchen chair.

She'd been right. She *was* stronger than she looked, because Leo wasn't small.

"Let's see," Finn said, giving the little boy a reassuring smile.

Leo shrank away and held his hand against his chest.

"I won't touch it. I just want to look." To Kayla he added, "I have first-aid training from the service. But it's probably fine. Your call."

"Let Mr. Finn look, honey. Let's count one-two-three and then do the hard thing. Ready?"

Leo looked up, leaned into her and nodded. "Okay."

Together, they counted. "One, two, three." And then Leo squeezed his eyes shut and held out his hand.

Finn studied the small hand, the superficial cut across two fingers. He opened his mouth to reassure Kayla and Leo.

And then memory crashed in.

He'd put a Band-Aid on Derek's hand, not long before the accident. He'd cuddled the boy to his chest as he held the little hand—just like Leo's—in his own larger one. Carefully squeezed the antibiotic on the small scrape, added a superhero Band-Aid and wiped his son's tears.

"It looks fine," he said to Kayla through a suddenly tight throat. "You go ahead and dress it." He shoved the materials at her, limped over to the window and looked out, trying to compose himself.

Normally, he kept a lid on his emotions about his son. Especially his son. Deirdre, yes, he grieved losing her, but she was an adult and she'd made a lot of bad choices that had contributed to her death.

His son had been an innocent victim.

"There. All fixed!" Kayla's voice was perky and up-beat. "You keep that Band-Aid on, now. Don't go showing that cut to your friends. It's a big one."

"It *is* big," Leo said, his voice steadying. "I was brave, wasn't I, Mommy?"

Finn turned back in time to see her hug him. "You were super brave. Good job."

Leo came over to Finn and, from a safe distance, held up his hand. "See? It was a really big cut!"

"It sure was," Finn said and then cleared the roughness out of his throat. "Sorry I don't have any fun Band-Aids. Not many kids come around here."

And there was a good reason for that. Having little boys around would tear him apart.

Change the subject. "You want to watch TV for a few minutes, buddy? I need to talk to your mom."

Leo's head jerked around to look at Kayla. "Can I, Mom?"

She hesitated. "I guess, for a few minutes. If we can find a decent show." She looked at Finn pointedly. "I actually don't allow him to watch much TV."

"Sorry." He headed into the living room and clicked the TV on, found a cartoonish-looking show that he remembered his son liking and looked at Kayla. "This okay?"

She squinted at the TV. "Yeah. Sure."

Her phone buzzed again, but she ignored it.

In the kitchen, she looked at him with two vertical lines between her eyebrows. "What's up?"

"Why'd you grill Long John about me?" he asked her abruptly.

At the sharp question from Finn, Kayla's mind reeled. "What do you mean?" she asked, buying time.

She knew exactly what he meant.

Long John must have gotten on the phone the moment she'd left his cabin. And wasn't that just like a soldier, to report anything and everything to his military buddies.

They're friends, an inner voice reminded her. She'd just met Long John, while Finn had probably known him for months if not years.

Finn let out a sigh. "Long John let me know you were asking all kinds of questions about me. I wondered why."

She studied him for signs of out-of-control anger and saw none. In which case, the best defense was a good offense. "You have a problem with me checking my employer's references the same way you and Penny are checking mine?" she bluffed.

He looked at her for a moment. "No. That's not a problem. It's just that some of your questions seemed pointed. All about my military service."

"That's part of your background," she said.

Finn shook his head. "I'm just not comfortable with having you here if you have any sort of attitude toward the military," he said. "The veterans are the most important thing to us, and believe it or not, they're sensitive. Especially the ones we get here. I don't need a worker who's cringing away from them or, on the other hand, overly curious."

She nodded. "That makes sense." She should have known this wouldn't work. It was too perfect.

The thought of going back on the road filled her with anxiety, though. Her supply of money was dwindling, and so was Leo's patience.

This place was *perfect* for Leo.

She tried to hang on to the pastor's words from this morning. What was the verse? *I know the plans I have for you…*

God has a plan for us.

She straightened her spine. "We'll get our things together tonight and move on tomorrow."

Her phone buzzed for about the twentieth time. Impatient, she pulled it out. She read through the texts from her friend Janice, back in Arkansas, her anxiety growing.

Don't come back under any circumstances.
He tore up your place.
He's raving that he's going to find you.
Get a PFA, fast.

She sank into a kitchen chair, her hand pressed to her mouth, her heart pounding. What was she going to do now?

"Listen, Kayla, I didn't mean you had to leave this minute," Finn said. "You can stay out the week, like we discussed. We can even help you figure out your next step. I just don't think…" He paused.

There was a brisk knock at the screen door, and then Penny walked in. "I called the last reference, and they raved about you," she said to Kayla. "So as far as I'm concerned, you're hired."

Kayla glanced up at Finn in time to see his forehead wrinkle. "Temporarily," he said.

"Long-term, as far as I'm concerned." Penny gave him an even stare.

"We need to talk," he said to Penny.

"All right." She put a bunch of paper in front of Kayla. "Start signing," she said. "Look for the *X*s."

Finn and Penny went out onto the porch, and she heard the low, intense sound of an argument.

From the living room, she heard Leo laughing at the television.

Finn didn't want to hire her. That was clear, and it wasn't only because she'd been nosy. Something else about her bothered him.

Which was fine, because he kind of bothered her, too. She didn't think he was dangerous himself, but he was clearly linked up to the veteran old boys' network. If Mitch started yelling at one of his meetings about how they were missing, the word could get out. Paratroopers were intensely loyal and they helped each other out, and a missing child would definitely be the type of thing that would stir up their interest and sympathy.

She needed to be farther away, but for now, the protection offered by the ranch was probably the safest alternative for Leo. A week, two, even a month here would give her breathing room.

Or maybe Mitch's rage would burn out. Although it hadn't in the year since the divorce he'd fought every inch of the way.

Finn didn't want her here, but she was used to that. She'd grown up in a home where she wasn't wanted.

And Penny had seemed to intuit some of her issues when Kayla had probed about Finn and the ranch during a lull before the church service. She'd said something about men, how women needed to stick together. Penny was on her side.

She could deal with Finn. She didn't need his approval or his smiles.

And she didn't want to depend on anyone. But here, she could work hard, pull her weight.

Finn and Penny came back in. Finn's jaw jutted out. Penny looked calm.

"You can have the job," Finn said.

"However long you want it," Penny added, glancing over at Finn.

Kayla drew in a deep breath, looking at them. "Thank you."

Then, her insides quivering, she picked up the pen and started signing.

Chapter Four

Finn headed for the kennels around eight o'clock the next morning, enjoying the sight of the Sangre de Cristos. He could hear the dogs barking and the whinnying of a horse. They only kept two, and Penny cared for them up at the small barn, but she sometimes took one out for a little ride in the morning.

Up ahead, Kayla's cabin door opened, and she and Leo came out.

He frowned. He wasn't thrilled about her working here, but he was resigned to it. He just had to stay uninvolved, that was all.

He watched her urge Leo into the car. Leo resisted, turning away as if to run toward the cabin, but she caught him in a bear hug.

Uh-oh. Wherever they were going—probably down to the church day camp—Leo wasn't on board.

She set Leo down and pointed at the back seat, and with obvious reluctance, the boy climbed in. Through the car's open windows, he heard Leo complain, "I can't get it buckled."

She bent over and leaned in, and he noticed she didn't

raise her voice even though Leo continued to whine. She spoke soothingly but didn't give in.

Finn looked away and tried to think about something other than what it would be like to parent a kid Leo's age.

Derek's age.

When she tried to start the car, all that happened was some loud clicking and grinding. A wisp of smoke wafted from the front of the vehicle.

She got out and raised the hood. From inside the car, Leo's voice rose. "If I have to go, I don't want to be late!"

By now, Finn had reached the point where her cabin's little driveway intersected with the road. He looked out over the valley and sniffed the aromatic pines and tried to stay uninvolved. She hadn't seen him. He could walk on by.

He tried to. Stopped. "Need a jump?"

She bit her lip, its fullness at odds with her otherwise plain looks and too-thin figure. She looked from him to Leo. As clear as the brightening blue sky, he could see the battle between her desire for independence and her child's needs.

"I think my starter's bad."

"You need to call for a tow?" He stood beside her and pretended to know what he was looking at. Truth was, despite the fact that he'd sold farm machinery in one of his jobs, car repair wasn't in his skill set.

She shook her head. "I can fix it, if I can get down to town and get the part."

He looked sideways at her. "You sure?"

She blew out a *pfft* of air and nodded. "Sure. Just

takes a screwdriver and a couple of bolts. Trouble is, Leo needs to get to camp."

His glance strayed to her mouth again but he looked away quickly, glancing down to the cross around her neck. She wasn't a girl up for grabs, obviously, and even if she were, he couldn't partake. One, because she was sort of his employee—Penny was technically her boss, but he was her direct supervisor. And two, because of what he'd done. He didn't deserve to connect with a woman. He needed to remember his decision in that regard.

No one had ever tested it before, not really.

But there was nothing wrong with giving her and the boy a ride, was there? Any Good Samaritan would do that.

"I planned to head down into town anyway," he said. "I can move up my schedule. Come on. Grab his booster seat and we'll hop in my truck."

She hesitated and looked toward Leo, who appeared very small even in the compact car. "Okay. Thank you. That would be a big help." She leaned in. "Hustle out, buddy. Mr. Finn's going to give us a ride."

"Is our car broken?"

"Yes, but I can fix it," she said, her voice confident.

Leo nodded. "Okay."

Finn carried the booster seat and Kayla held Leo's hand as they walked down the dirt road toward Finn's place and the truck. The piney breeze felt fresh against his face. A mountain bluebird flashed by, chirping its *TOO-too, TOO-too.*

Other than that, it was quiet, because Kayla wasn't a person who had to talk all the time. As a quiet man himself, he appreciated that.

The ride to town got too quiet, though, so he turned on a little country music. When his current favorite song came on, he saw her tapping a hand against her jean-clad thigh. He was tapping the steering wheel, same rhythm, and when their eyes met, she flashed a smile.

They got close to town, and there was a sniffling sound in the back seat. Kayla turned half-around. "What's wrong, buddy?"

"I don't want to go." Leo's voice trembled.

"It's hard to do new things," she said, her voice matter-of-fact.

"My tummy hurts."

"Sometimes that happens when you're scared." She paused, then added, "Anyone would be a little bit afraid, meeting a lot of new people. But we know how to do things anyway, even when we're scared."

"I don't want to." His voice dripped misery.

The tone and the sound brought back Finn's son, hard. He remembered taking Derek to his first T-ball practice, a new team of kids he didn't know. Finn had comforted him in the same way Kayla was comforting Leo.

His breath hitched. He needed to stop making that dumb kind of equation. "You'd better stop crying," he said to Leo. "Buck up. The other boys will laugh at you."

Finn looked in the rearview mirror, saw the boy's narrow shoulders cringe and wanted to knock himself in the head.

Leo drew in a sharp, hiccupy breath.

Kayla was giving Finn the death stare. "Anyone worth being your friend will understand if you're a little scared the first day," she said over her shoulder.

But Leo kept gasping in air, trying to get his tears

under control. And that *was* good; the other kids wouldn't like a crybaby, but still. Finn had no right to tell Leo what to do.

No rights in this situation, at all.

And now the tension in the truck was thicker than an autumn fog.

He'd created the problem and he needed to fix it. "Hey," he said, "when do you want the dog to come live with you?"

The snuffly sounds stopped. Kayla glanced back at Leo, then at Finn, her eyes narrowed.

He could tell she was debating whether or not to trust him and go along with this or to stay angry. He'd seen that expression plenty of times before, with his wife. She'd have chosen to hold on to her anger, no question.

"I don't know." Kayla put on a thoughtful voice. "I'd rather wait until this evening when Leo's home from camp. That way, he can help me handle her. That is…" She turned half-around again. "Do you think we're ready to take care of a dog? You'd have to help me."

"Yeah!" Leo's voice was loud and excited. "I know we can do it, Mom."

"Hey, Leo," Finn said, "I don't know the dog's name. She needs a new one. Maybe the other kids at camp could help you pick one out." Actually, the former owners *had* told Finn the dog's name. It was a common curse word. Even now, thinking of their nasty laughs as they'd dumped the eager, skinny, blind-and-deaf dog at the ranch, his mouth twisted.

"Okay!" Leo said as they pulled into the church parking lot. "I'll ask them what we should name her!" He unfastened his seat belt as soon as the truck stopped, clearly eager to get on with his day.

"Wait a minute," Kayla warned Leo as he reached for the door handle. "I need to take you in, and we have to walk on the lines in the parking lot. It's for safety. The teacher told me when I talked to her."

"I'll be here," Finn said as Kayla got nimbly out of the truck and then opened the back for Leo to jump down. They walked toward the building holding hands, Leo walking beside her, moving more slowly as they got closer.

Watching them reminded him of dropping off his son.

He couldn't make a practice of getting involved with Kayla and Leo, he told himself sternly. It hurt too much. And it gave his heart crazy ideas about the possibility of having a family sometime in the future.

That wasn't happening, his head reminded him.

But his heart didn't seem to be listening.

Kayla walked out of the church after dropping Leo off at the camp program, her stomach twisting and tears pressing at her eyes.

If only she didn't have to start him in a new program so soon after arriving in town. But she had to work; there wasn't a choice about that.

He'll be fine. He has to grow up sometime.

But he'd looked so miserable.

The lump in her throat grew and the tears overflowed.

To her mortification, two of the other mothers—or maybe it was a mother and a grandmother—noticed and came over. "What's wrong, honey?" the older, red-headed one asked.

The younger woman came to her other side and startled Kayla by wrapping her in a hug. "Are you okay?"

What kind of a town was this, where complete strangers hugged you when you were sad? Kayla pulled back as soon as she graciously could and nodded. "I just hate...leaving him...in a new place."

"Gotcha," the older woman said without judgment and handed her a little packet of tissues. "I'm Marge. Just dropped off my Brenna in the same classroom your boy was in. It's a real good program."

Kayla drew in big gasps of air. "I'm sorry." She blew her nose. "I feel like an idiot."

"Oh, I know what you're going through," the mother who'd hugged her said. "I cried every single day of the first two weeks at kindergarten drop-off." She patted Kayla's shoulder. "I'm Missy, by the way. What's your name? I haven't seen you around."

"I'm Kayla. Pleased to meet you." She got the words out without crying any more, but barely.

"Now, me," Marge said, "I jumped for joy when Brenna started kindergarten. She's my sixth," she added, "and I love her to pieces, but it was the first time I had the house to myself in fifteen years. I don't want to give up the freedom come summer, so all my kids are in some kind of program or sport."

Kayla tried to smile but couldn't. Leo had gone willingly enough with the counselor in charge, no doubt buoyed up by the prospect of telling the other children he was getting a dog. But as they'd walked away, he'd shot such a sad, plaintive look over his shoulder. That was what had done her in.

For a long time, it had been her and Leo against the world. She had to learn to let him go, let him grow up, but she didn't have to like it.

In the past year of starting and running her little

business, cleaning houses for wealthy people, she'd paid attention to how they cared for their kids. Lots of talking, lots of book reading. That had been easy for her to replicate with Leo.

A couple of the families she'd really admired had given their kids independence and decision-making power, even at a fairly young age. That was harder for Kayla to do, given how she and Leo had been living, though she could see the merits of it. "Maybe I should go back in and check on him," she said, thinking aloud.

"Don't do it," Missy advised. "You'll just make yourself miserable. And if he sees you, he'll get more upset."

"He'll be fine." Marge waved a hand. "They have your number to call you if there's anything wrong. Enjoy the time to yourself."

One of the other mothers, a tall, beautifully made-up blonde, drifted over. "Some of us are going to Flexible Coffee for a bit," she said to Kayla. "I noticed you're new. Want to come?"

More small-town friendliness? Kayla appreciated it, but she didn't quite feel comfortable. She didn't want to go socialize for an hour or two; she had a car starter to buy and install.

Before she could beg off, Marge lifted an eyebrow and pinned the woman with a steady stare. "Glad you're willing to bury the hatchet, Sylvie—that is, if you're inviting all of us. You haven't spoken to me since Brenna gave Jocelyn that surprise haircut last year."

Sylvie shuddered. "Right before she had a pageant. She could have won."

Marge snorted. "Don't pin that on me. Jocelyn wears a wig to those things, just like every other little beauty queen."

"I wouldn't expect *you* to understand." Sylvie's once-over, taking in Marge's faded T-shirt and cutoff shorts, wasn't subtle.

Missy rolled her eyes. "Would you two stop fighting? You're going to give Kayla here a bad impression of our town."

The gorgeous Sylvie glanced out into the parking lot and then looked at Kayla speculatively. "That looked like Finn Gallagher's truck. Are you two seeing each other?"

"No!" Heat climbed Kayla's cheeks. All three women looked at her and she realized she'd spoken too loudly. "I work for him, that's all," she said quickly, trying to sound casual. "I'm having car trouble, so he gave me and my son a ride to town."

"Think I'll go say hello." Sylvie sashayed over to Finn's truck.

"One of these days, she's going to land him," Marge said.

"Not sure she's his type," Missy said.

"Long-legged blondes are every guy's type." Marge stretched. "You two going to take her up on her coffee invite?"

"I have to work," Missy said, turning toward the row of cars. "But if you go, call me later with all the gossip, okay?"

"Will do," Marge called after her. Then she turned to Kayla. "How about you. Want to come?"

"I have to work, too." And Kayla wasn't sure she wanted to get in the middle of a lot of gossip. Back in high school, she'd envied the girls who knew everything about everyone and felt comfortable in the spotlight, but no more.

Now she just wanted peace. And peace, for her, definitely meant staying *out* of the spotlight.

"Well, it was nice meeting you. Think I'll go just to see what news Sylvie's gathered," Marge added. "Unless she decides to hook up with Finn right here and now." She nodded toward Finn's truck.

Sylvie had propped her crossed arms on the open window and was leaning in. She ran a hand through her long blond hair, flipping it back.

Kayla felt a surge of the old jealousy. There were women who stood out and got noticed. And then there were women like her. As good-looking as Finn Gallagher was, he'd definitely go for the showier type.

Which didn't matter, of course. Finn could date whomever he chose, and it wasn't her business. She just hoped he could still give her a ride back to the ranch before taking off with Sylvie.

But Sylvie backed away quickly, spun and headed toward the main parking lot where Kayla and Marge still stood.

"Did you get a date?" Marge asked her bluntly.

"Marge! And no. He blew me off again." Sylvie sighed dramatically. "If only I didn't have this attraction to unavailable men. Are we going for coffee or not?"

"I'll meet you over there," Marge said.

"How about you, Kayla?" Sylvie studied her a little too hard. "Come on—join us. I'd like to get to know you."

No way. "Thank you," she said in the fake-nice voice women like Sylvie always inspired in her. "I appreciate the coffee offer, but I really do need to get going. Thank you for helping me with my meltdown," she added to Marge. "I'll see you at pickup, or maybe another day this week. 'Bye, Sylvie."

She hurried off toward Finn's truck, hoping she hadn't been too abrupt.

"What went on just now?" Finn asked as soon as she'd settled inside and fastened her seat belt.

She shrugged. "They asked me for coffee, but I told them I needed to work."

"You know, your shift doesn't start until ten. You could've gone."

"No, thanks."

He looked at her speculatively but didn't ask any questions. "I'd like to take you to breakfast," he said instead.

That jolted her inner alarm system but good. "Why?"

"Because I'm guessing you haven't eaten, and you have a long day of work ahead." He hesitated, then added, "And because I upset Leo, and I want to make it up to you."

"That's not necessary. You fixed it." What did he want with her, inviting her to a meal?

He must have read her wariness, because he spread his hands. "No big deal. I often stop at the Peak View Diner for breakfast. It's cheap, and Long John and Willie will probably be there. They'd love to have a new audience."

Oh. Well, if Long John and Willie would be there…

"Best bacon biscuits in the state." He offered a winning smile that made her breath catch.

Her stomach growled. "Well…"

"Look," he said, "I'm not asking you out, if that's what's worrying you. It's just that Esperanza Springs is a sociable little town. People are curious about you, and it's better for them to meet you than to gossip among themselves."

"Bacon biscuits, huh?" She grinned and lifted her hands, palms up. "I can't turn that down. Just as long as you and Long John and Willie protect me from the gossip hounds."

"Believe me," he said, "nobody can get a word in around those guys' stories, but they really are popular. If people see you're with them—"

"And with you?" she interrupted.

"To a lesser extent, yes. So we'll make an appearance, eat a couple of biscuits and then get back to the peace and solitude I think we both prefer."

She looked at him sideways and gave a slow nod. "Okay," she said and then looked away, afraid of revealing the surge of emotion that had welled up in her at his words.

It wasn't that often that people paid enough attention to Kayla to figure out what she was like inside. And it was even less often that someone shared the same preferences and tastes.

Unfortunately, Kayla was finding Finn's attention and understanding just a little bit too appealing.

That night, Kayla spooned up another sloppy joe for Leo. She sat back in her chair at the little table, pushed her own empty plate away and stretched.

Despite her sore muscles and tiredness, she had a sense of accomplishment.

Working in the kennel had been physical and sometimes hard, but she loved the sweet old dogs already. And she was relieved to know that she could do the work, that it wasn't too hard for her. Finn's directions were clear and easy to understand, and he'd left her to do her job rather than hovering over her.

After work, she'd put the new starter in her car. *Thank you, online videos.* Paying someone to fix something simple like that just wasn't in the budget.

She looked around the bare cabin. That might be her next project, making it look a little homier.

It would be a while before she found a spare hour to dig out her old camera and explore the ranch, take some shots. She was an amateur, but she enjoyed photography. Living in such a beautiful place was making her itch to capture some images.

But for today, she'd gotten the car fixed and dinner on the table and started a job, and that was enough. She'd sleep well tonight.

Leo wiped a napkin across his face and chattered on about his day at camp, his new friends and potential names for the dog. She didn't have the heart to correct him for talking with his mouth full. Fortunately, he seemed to have forgotten that Finn had said he'd bring the dog around tonight, because that didn't seem to be happening.

Or maybe he was just used to men disappointing him, as Mitch had so many times when he'd failed to pick Leo up for visits as planned.

We're free from all that now. She pushed thoughts of her ex away. Instead, she listened to her son chatter and let her shoulders relax, stretching her neck from side to side. She'd better get these dinner dishes washed before she got so sleepy she was tempted to just let it go. This cabin was way too small for that, especially since the kitchen, dining room and living room were just one connected space.

There was a knock on the door, a little scuffling.

Her shoulders tensed again.

"It's Finn, with a special visitor," came the deep voice that was already becoming familiar to her.

"The *dog*!" Leo shouted and jumped up from the table. "May I be 'scused?"

"You may." She smiled and stood up.

Leo ran to the door and flung it open. "Hi, dog!"

"She's here for you if you're ready," Finn said to Kayla, restraining the black cocker spaniel just inside the doorway. "If not, tonight can just be a visit."

Kayla laughed and rubbed Leo's back. "You think you'll be able to get her out of here again? We're as ready as we'll ever be." She knelt down, and Finn dropped the leash, and the dog walked right into her arms.

"She's so sweet!" Kayla rubbed her sides and turned a little, encouraging the dog to go to Leo, who reached out to hug her tight.

"Gentle!" Kayla laughed as the dog gave Leo a brief lick. "Let her go and we'll see what she does."

The dog started to explore, keeping her nose to the floor as she trotted around. She bumped into a kitchen chair, backed up and continued on her quest as if nothing had happened.

When she reached Leo again, she was ready to examine him. She licked his hands and face while he squealed and laughed.

Kayla laughed, too. "Leo must smell like dinner," she said and then looked up at Finn. "Would you like a plate? We have plenty of sloppy joes and corn on the cob." She flushed a little as she named the humble fare. Finn was probably used to better.

Finn looked over at the table, and for a moment something like longing flashed across his face. But it was gone so quickly that she might have imagined it. "It does smell good," he said, "but I already ate with Penny and a couple of the guys. We do meals together occasionally."

Leo rolled away from the friendly dog, and she knelt in a play bow and uttered a couple of short barks.

"She's deaf, but she still barks?" Kayla asked.

"She's not entirely deaf. And she barks when she's excited." He ruffled Leo's hair. "She's excited now. I think she likes you."

Leo looked up at Finn, eyes positively glowing.

Finn slid a backpack off and set it on the floor. "If you're sure you're ready, I'll get out her stuff."

Kayla nodded. "That's fine. I'm just going to get the dinner dishes cleaned up." She hoped Finn would pick up on the fact that she wanted Leo to be as involved as possible.

He seemed to read her mind. "Leo, I need help," Finn said. "If you can just let the dog explore for a few minutes, we'll get out her supplies."

"Supplies?" Leo's eyes widened.

Finn pulled out a food dish and large water bowl. "Now, the thing about dogs and food," he said to Leo, "is that you never want to come between them. This one's gentle, but she's been hungry before and she probably remembers it. Dogs can get a little bit mad if they think you're taking their food."

Kayla couldn't resist: she walked over and knelt to hear the lesson. The dishes could wait.

"Did you choose a new name for her?" Finn asked.

"Shoney," Leo said, looking up at Kayla. "It's the place where my dad and me liked to go for dinner."

Kayla stared blankly at her son. She hadn't realized that was why he liked the name. And wasn't it amazing that a kid could love a dad as mean and inattentive as Mitch had been? He'd taken Leo out for a meal exactly once since the divorce.

If Finn felt those undercurrents, he ignored them. Instead he continued with the lesson, explaining the leash and the toys and the brush for the dog's hair.

Kayla's shoulders relaxed. Finn was a steady man. He'd arrived when he'd said, bringing the dog, bringing the supplies they needed. He showed Leo how to gently lead Shoney around so that she didn't get hurt running into things. He pulled out a blanket, ragged but clean, and explained that it was the blanket Shoney had been using in the kennel, and would help her feel more comfortable in a new place.

"I used to have a blanket," Leo said, "but we put it away." He hesitated, then added, "I only use it sometimes. In 'mergencies."

Finn nodded. "Makes sense."

Finn wasn't like other men she'd known, her mother's boyfriends or the teasing boys at school, or Mitch. In fact, she'd never met a man like him before.

He glanced over, and she flushed and looked away. She focused on the paneled walls, the curtainless windows, through which she could see the sun turning the tops of the mountains red, making the pasturelands golden. Crisp evening air came through the screen door, a welcome coolness for her warm face.

Leo filled the dog bowl with water and set it in the

corner on a towel just as Finn had instructed, pausing often to pat Shoney. Then he returned to the backpack to check out the rest of Shoney's supplies.

"Your son's careful," Finn said approvingly.

"He's had to be." Unbidden, a memory from Leo's younger days pushed into her awareness.

Leo had just turned four, and he'd spilled a glass of juice at the table. Just a few drops had hit Mitch's phone before Kayla had swooped in with a towel, but he'd jumped up, shouted at Leo and raised his fist.

She'd intercepted the blow, but her heart still broke thinking of how Leo had tried to stifle his tears.

"Look, Mom!" His voice now was worlds away from that fearful one, and happiness bloomed inside her.

"What do you have there?" She stood and walked over to him.

"There's a scarf for her!" He held up a pink-checked neckerchief.

"Cool! See how it looks on her."

As Leo crossed the room to where Shoney had flopped down, Kayla looked over at Finn. "You dress your dogs?" she asked teasingly, lifting an eyebrow.

He shrugged and a dimple appeared in his cheek. His gaze stayed fixed on hers. "I like a girl in nice clothes."

"Oh, you do?"

They looked at each other for a moment more, until several realizations dawned on Kayla at once.

She was flirting. She *never* flirted.

She didn't have nice clothes, another fact that put Finn out of her league.

And this situation, living in close proximity to Finn here at the ranch, could get out of control all too easily.

She looked away from him, her cheeks heating.

No surprise that he turned and walked over to Leo, ensuring that their slightly romantic moment was over. "Here's a scoop for dog food," he explained while Kayla finished clearing up the dinner dishes. "She gets one scoop in the morning and one in the evening."

"How can Shoney find her food, if she's blind?" Leo asked.

"Because of her super sense of smell," Finn explained, then put a piece of food on the floor near Shoney. Sure enough, the shaggy black dog found it almost immediately.

Kayla's heart melted, not in a flirty way now, but in a grateful way. As Leo experimented with having Shoney find bits of food, she walked over to Finn and knelt beside him to watch.

"He's being gentle," Finn said. "You've taught him well."

That meant the world to Kayla, for someone to say she'd done a good job. Especially on gentleness, since his male role model had been anything but. "You're really good with him yourself," she said. "Have you spent a lot of time around kids?"

All the joy drained out of Finn's face. He looked away, then rose smoothly to his feet and picked up his now-empty backpack. "You good for now?" he asked, his voice gruff.

"Um, sure. I think so." What had she said wrong?

"Then I'll leave you alone with your new family member. See you, Leo." Finn was out the door almost before Leo could offer a wave.

As she petted the dog and helped Leo get to know her, she mused over the encounter in her mind. It was when she'd mentioned kids that he'd closed off.

There was some kind of story there. And God help her, but she wanted to know it.

Chapter Five

The next morning, Kayla tried not to notice Finn's very muscular arms as he pulled the truck into a parking lot in town, just beneath the Esperanza Springs Fourth of July Community Celebration banner.

"Like I said, I'm sorry to make you work on a holiday," Finn said, in the same friendly but utterly impersonal tone he'd taken all morning. "But once we get the dogs settled, you can hang out with Leo and do whatever, until the parade starts." He was acting differently toward her, after the awkward ending to their evening last night. She'd replayed it in her mind, and she didn't think she'd said anything to offend him. Maybe he was just moody. Or maybe she was imagining his distance.

Trying to match his businesslike cordiality, she gave him a quick, impersonal smile as she climbed down from the truck and got Leo out of the back. "No problem. I think it'll be a fun day."

"Will Shoney be okay?" Leo asked. He'd been loath to leave her alone, and truthfully, Kayla had felt the same. Shoney had followed them to the door, and when

Kayla had nudged her back inside so she could close it, the dog had cried mournfully.

Finn nodded down at Leo. "Shoney's been staying in a little cage in the kennel for a few weeks. She'll be thrilled to have your whole cabin to herself for a little while."

Kayla focused on the intensely blue sky and the bright sun that illuminated the broad, flat valley, framed by the Sangre de Cristos. Even on the prettiest summer day in Arkansas, the air didn't have this refreshing crispness to it. "Come on," she said to Leo. "Let's go find Miss Penny. She said you could hang around with her while Mom works."

"Okay," he said agreeably, and Kayla sent up a prayer of thanks for Leo's accepting, nonconfrontational demeanor.

They didn't have far to look, because as soon as they'd turned toward the celebration's central area, Penny approached them. "Hey, Leo, I think they've got some good fry bread for breakfast. Have you ever had Native American food?"

Leo looked up at Kayla, puzzled.

"No, he hasn't," Kayla said to Penny, "and neither have I. But we're both in favor of bread and fried food, so I'm sure he'll love it."

"Come on, kiddo. Let's go!" And the two were off into the small line of food vendors, most still setting up, along the edge of the town park.

Kayla helped Finn lift down the crates. They'd brought five dogs, well-socialized ones who could handle the crowds and noise, healthy ones more likely to be adopted.

"We'll put them in the shade, out of the way, and let them out one at a time to move around and get some exercise. If you can stay and do that while I park the truck, there won't be that much more to do."

So she let each dog out and strolled around, keeping them leashed but letting them greet people politely. It would be great if all five found homes today.

Suddenly, Axel, the ancient rottweiler Kayla was walking, started barking and pulling at the leash. Kayla got him under control as the other dogs chimed in, barking from their crates. She looked around to see what was causing the ruckus.

Two women walked in their direction, each with two large Alaskan malamutes on leashes. It took a minute, but Kayla recognized the taller woman as Marge from the previous day's camp drop-off.

She stood still as the pair slowly approached, keeping Axel close and smiling a greeting. And then she saw the lettering on Marge's shirt, identical to that of the other woman: Mountain Malamutes.

"We breed 'em," the other woman explained, gathering both of her leashes in one hand and leaning forward to greet Kayla. "I'm Rosa. We're teaming up with you and Finn today to try and get your guys adopted."

"Great, but how?" Kayla was struggling to keep Axel from pulling her off her feet and to speak above the noise of the crated dogs. Meanwhile, the malamutes stood panting, tongues out, alert but quiet. "And how on earth do you get your dogs to behave so well?"

Marge laughed. "Thousands of years of breeding, for starters," she said. "They're work dogs. Plus, we train 'em hard. But Rosa and I, we feel bad about breeding dogs when there are so many rescues who need homes, so we help where we can."

A group of men in Western shirts walked by, most

carrying musical instruments, and Kayla recognized Long John's shuffling gait. Willie was beside him, and the two stopped and greeted Kayla as if they'd known her for years instead of days.

"You and young Leo should come hear us play," Willie said, patting her arm.

"That you should," Long John agreed. "We're at eleven and then again at three, right over on the stage they're setting up." He waved a hand toward a flurry of activity at the center of the park.

"I will," Kayla promised, warmed by their friendliness.

As the men walked on, a little girl about Leo's size rushed over and wrapped her arms around Marge's legs. "Mommy!" she cried, sounding upset. She buried her face in Marge's leg.

Marge extracted herself, knelt and studied the little girl's upset face. "What's wrong, baby?"

"Sissy and Jim won't play with me. So I got mad and ran away from them."

Marge's eyes narrowed as she scanned the area. "I'm gonna speak my piece to those two when I find 'em." She looked up at Kayla. "Two of my older kids. They're supposed to be taking care of Brenna."

"Hi, Brenna," Kayla said, smiling at the adorable little redhead. "I think you were in camp with my son, Leo, yesterday."

"Uh-huh." Brenna sucked a finger. "We played on the swings."

"Matter of fact," Marge said, "I think I see him right over there on the playground. Want to run over and see if he wants to play?" Marge turned to Kayla. "Is that okay?"

"I'm sure it is. Let me just text Penny." She did, and the answer came back immediately: Send her over. The more, the merrier.

Brenna took off for the play area, and when she got there, she hugged Leo. And then they started climbing a multilevel wooden structure.

A volley of rapid Spanish rang out nearby, and Hector, the boy who'd played with Leo at church, ran to join Leo and Brenna.

Kayla's breath caught as gratitude swept over her. Some small towns could be clannish, but Esperanza Springs had welcomed her and Leo with open arms.

She was well on her way to falling in love with this place. The natural beauty and the distance from Arkansas were great, but more than that, she already felt like part of a community.

Moments later, Finn returned, in time to direct another truck their way. Then they all helped unload five empty dog crates on wheels, made to look like circus animal carts, but cunningly arranged with harnesses. As Finn and Rosa tested out one of the carts, hooking up a malamute and putting in Charcoal, the largest dog they'd brought from the ranch, Kayla couldn't help clapping her hands. "That's so adorable!"

Marge nodded. "Exactly the reaction we're looking for. And the next step we're hoping for is that people who get swept away with the cuteness will want to adopt the dog."

"And buy a malamute," Rosa called.

"It's a win-win." Finn adjusted the cart, and they all watched while the malamute trotted in a circle, tail and ears high, pulling the silver-muzzled Lab mix.

"It's working. If it works for Charcoal, it'll work for

all the dogs." Finn let Charcoal out of the cart and urged him back into his crate. "Kayla, if you want to take some time off, you're welcome. I'd just need a little assistance at twelve thirty, when the parade's lining up."

"Thanks, boss." She added a sassy smile, forgetting for a moment to be businesslike and keep her distance.

He lifted an eyebrow, the corners of his own mouth turning up.

Kayla forced herself to turn away. She strolled through the grounds, savoring the sights, smells and sounds of a small-town Fourth of July. She'd grown up in Little Rock, and if the city had offered such events back then, her mother hadn't known about them. She and Mitch had taken Leo to a few Fourth of July gatherings, but the kind Mitch favored involved a lot of drinking. They didn't have this wholesome feel.

"Hey." Sylvie, the pretty blonde who'd issued the coffee invite the day before, fell into step beside her. "How's it going? Having fun with our Podunk event?"

"I love it, actually," Kayla said.

"Is your son here?" Sylvie looked sideways at her.

"Yes. He's on the playground." Kayla reached up and ran her fingers along the soft, low branches of a cottonwood tree, enjoying the ambling freedom of walking through the park.

"Hey, listen," Sylvie said. "I know Finn seems like a nice guy, but you should be careful. Especially being a single mom and all."

Kayla straightened. "Why?"

Sylvie looked at her like she was dense. "Well, because no one knows anything about his history, of course!" She opened her mouth as if to say more, but a handsome cowboy waved to her. "Gotta go," she said.

Kayla's walk slowed as she approached the playground. She replayed what Sylvie had said. Was there something she didn't know about Finn? Was he a risk?

That was hard to believe. He seemed safe and trustworthy.

So did Mitch. When they'd first started dating, he'd been so attentive that Kayla had felt like she was living in a fairy tale. Roses, candlelight dinners, unexpected visits just to tell her he was thinking of her. For a girl who'd felt like a mistake all her life, all that romance had been heady stuff. Accepting his proposal had been a no-brainer. He was the only man who'd ever seemed to care.

But even during their engagement, she'd started to feel a little constricted. She'd realized his love was possessive, probably too possessive. She'd told herself it was because he loved her, that at least he wasn't running around on her or burying himself in his work.

Everything had changed when they'd had Leo. Having to share her affections had brought out the crazy in Mitch. And rather than getting used to parenting, growing into it, he'd gotten worse and worse.

She hesitated and then walked over to where Penny was sitting, checking her phone and glancing up at the kids often.

"Thanks so much for watching him," she said. "Can I ask you something?"

"Sure."

"Is there something I should know about Finn? Something that would make me or Leo at risk around him?"

Penny frowned. "Not a thing. Why do you ask?"

"This other mom, Sylvie. She said I should be careful around Finn."

"Nope. He's fine. He..." Penny hesitated. "He's had some heartache in his past. Tragedy, really. But I wouldn't say he's dangerous."

Tragedy. She'd sensed that about him.

She trusted Penny. And the truth was, she trusted Finn.

Mostly.

"Mom!" Leo ran over and hugged her. "This is fun!" He grabbed her hand and pulled her toward the wooden climbing structure. "Watch how high I can go!"

He climbed rapidly to the lookout tower, and Kayla had to force herself to smile and wave rather than climb up herself and make him come down. He was growing up, and this was a safe place. She had to let him spread his wings and fly.

Then he shouted, "Dad!"

Kayla's heart stopped. What on earth? Could Mitch be here?

Leo scrambled down to the ground and she met him there, but before she could grab him, he ran, hard, across the park's grassy area.

She ran after him, arms and legs pumping almost as fast as her heart. She caught up with him at the same moment that he reached a man in military fatigues and a maroon Airborne beret.

Not Mitch. Just the same uniform.

"You're not..." Leo looked up and then backed off of the man. "You're not Daddy." His eyes filled with tears.

"Oh, honey." Kayla's fear turned to sadness for her son. Despite all Mitch's failings as a dad, he was all Leo knew.

"So this little one is an Airborne kid, is he?" The

soldier knelt. "Come on—want to try on my hat?" He put it on Leo's head.

"So cute!" Someone snapped a picture. Then another woman, who turned out to be the soldier's wife, took a photo of the soldier and Leo together.

Anxiety bloomed in Kayla's chest. She turned to the soldier's wife, trying to keep the first one in her sights. "What are the photos for?"

"Oh, do you want me to send them to you?" The woman smiled. "You must be his mom. I'm Freida."

Kayla hated to quell the friendliness, but safe was safe. "I don't like photos of my son to be out and about, actually. Would you mind deleting them?"

The woman stared. "I was only trying to be nice. I wasn't going to put them up online or anything."

"Of course. I'm sure you wouldn't. It's just… I'm sorry."

The woman clicked a couple of buttons on her phone. "There. Gone." Her voice was cool, and her meaningful glance toward her husband showed that there was going to be plenty of talk about this at the dinner table tonight.

Kayla shook off her concern, because Leo was crying. She knelt and put her arms around him. "What's wrong, honey?"

"I thought it was Daddy!"

"You miss him, don't you?"

"Yeah. When are we gonna see him?"

That was the question. "Remember how we talked about it. Daddy's not safe for us right now."

"But I miss him."

Her heart broke for a little boy whose father wasn't worthy of the name. But he'd always loom large in Leo's thoughts, just as her own parents did. "I'm sure he misses you, too," she said. It might be true. As damaged as Mitch was, he still had to have some human feeling for his flesh and blood. Didn't he? "I have an idea. Let's make a scrapbook of pictures of you and the things we're doing. Maybe later, we can send it to him."

Leo nodded, but he was slumped as they walked back across the park.

Fortunately, the presence of the malamutes and the parade cheered him up, and he seemed to forget his sadness as he watched the parade and helped with the dogs. Then they ate their fill of hot dogs and baked beans and potato chips.

Finn approached just as they were scooping up the last of their brownies and ice cream. "Looks good," he said.

"Sit down and join us?" she invited before thinking better of it.

"I'd like to, but I'd better not. Listen, Willie's driving the truck back with the dogs. Long John, too. Dogs don't do so well with fireworks. In fact, a lot of our guys, Willie included, don't like them, either."

"Fireworks?" Leo's eyes widened. "Daddy loved those!"

"Why wouldn't the guys…? Oh," she said as realization dawned.

"Right. The loud noises and flashing lights remind them of…" He hesitated and looked at Leo. "Of some bad things in their pasts."

She smiled to show her appreciation of his tact. He wanted to protect Leo from harsh realities, just like she did. It was breathtakingly different from being with Mitch. And whatever Sylvie said, Kayla felt that Finn was basically a good guy.

"I want to stay for the fireworks, Mom. I miss Daddy."

She bit her lip. What would be the harm in staying?

"I'm meeting with some of my fellow Airborne Rangers," Finn said. "I'll drive back probably around eleven."

Right. She had to remember, and keep remembering, that Finn was loyal to his own kind. Not to her.

Also, she didn't need for Leo to be getting more memories of Mitch, becoming more unhappy and discontent. "I think we'll go ahead and leave with Willie," she decided.

"No!" Leo jumped up and kicked the picnic table, hard. "Ow!" he cried, obviously feeling the blow through his thin sneakers, the word ending in a wail as he plopped down on the ground to hold his foot. "I wanna stay for fireworks! Daddy would let me!"

She blew out a sigh. This day, that had started out so nicely, was going rapidly downhill. And she didn't know if she was making the right decisions. Didn't know if she was keeping him safer or sending him to the psychiatrist's couch. That was the problem of being a single parent: there was no one to consult with.

She dearly longed to consult with Finn, who was watching sympathetically as she patted Leo's shoulder and studied his foot to make sure he hadn't really hurt himself.

But she had to remember that Finn wasn't someone she should get close to, because his loyalty would inevitably be toward his military brothers, not a civilian woman and child.

Sighing, she turned her back on Leo and walked a few steps away, denying him the attention he was seeking. Finn nodded once and left the scene, too. He understood that much, at least, and she was grateful.

Leo's crying turned to hiccups and then stopped, and she turned back to him and held out a hand. "Come on. Let's go get in the car with the dogs and Mr. Willie. We'll see how Shoney's doing and take her for a walk." As she'd hoped, the idea of their new dog distracted Leo.

As for Kayla, she wished for all the world that she could stay and simply enjoy the warmth and fun of a small-town holiday.

The next Saturday, Finn came outside and was surprised to see Kayla laughing, standing close to a tall man whose back was turned. Even with her hair in its usual messy braid, she looked beautiful.

In the yard in front of the main house, Leo played with two little girls.

His chest tightened, and he had to force himself not to clench his fists. He started toward the pair, then stopped to take a calming look at the countryside, the flat basin surrounded by white-capped mountains.

Kayla wasn't his, no way. And he had no right to feel jealous that she was spending time with someone else.

He drew in a breath and continued on down. Halfway there, he recognized the pastor.

Which didn't necessarily make him feel any better. Carson Blair was good-looking and well respected, the father of twins just a bit older than Leo. He wasn't such a hulk as Finn, so he and Kayla were better matched physically.

More than that, the pastor wasn't carrying the load of guilt Finn did. On the contrary, he was a good man, a servant of God who had every right to happiness.

All of those logical thoughts didn't stop Finn's feet from moving toward them to see what was going on.

"Hey, Finn," the pastor said, smiling. "We've had an offer of some fishing. Would you like to join us?"

"An offer from whom?" He knew he sounded grouchy. "You need to sign a waiver if your kids are visiting the ranch. Liability issues."

"Didn't even think of that." The pastor gave an easy smile. "Where do I sign?"

Kayla was looking at him, confusion on her face. "Willie invited him, and Leo, too," she said. "He said he's had his grandkids fishing at the pond here. I didn't think you'd mind."

She was wearing her typical kennel uniform, jeans and a T-shirt. As usual, it made her look like a teenager.

It also meant she wasn't dressing up for the pastor. "No problem, just covering our backs," Finn said. "The ranch can't afford a lawsuit."

Kayla gave him a look as if to say that Carson Blair was hardly going to sue them. "I'll go get the waiver. Isn't Penny in the office?"

"Good idea."

That left him standing alone with Carson. "How are the girls?" he asked, just to avoid an awkward silence and the pastor's know-too-much eyes.

"They're doing pretty well. Life's a scramble, though. It sounded nice to come up here and relax for a little while. Get out some of their energy."

Leo chose that moment to glance over. He'd been shouting, but when he saw Finn, he lowered his voice.

Just the effect he wished he didn't have on kids. Although it *was* a useful reminder. Kids might not know exactly *why* he was scary, but they were right to be scared. He wasn't safe to be around.

Kayla came back, forking fingers through her hair with one hand while holding out the waiver with the other. In the past week, her bruises had faded to the point where she let her arms show. Finn could still see them, though. It reminded him that she'd been through a lot and didn't need him adding to her problems.

After the pastor had signed the waiver and run it back inside, they all headed down toward the pond where Willie was waiting, several fishing rods in hand.

"Okay, kids," Willie said, clearly in his element. "I'm going to give you each a fishing pole and show you how to bait it."

"With *worms*?" Carson's daughter—Skye, maybe?—stared into a Styrofoam container, horrified fascination on her face. The other twin and Leo peeked in, too, and a lively discussion broke out, amiably moderated by Willie.

Finn strolled away from the group. Just the smell of the lake, the fresh air, the smile on the old man's face, helped him get some perspective.

He was still raw from losing his wife and child, and probably always would be. What he wasn't used to was developing any kind of feelings for another woman and child. This was the first time his heart had come out of hibernation.

There were bound to be some missteps, some difficulties. He'd made the decision not to get involved again, but it had never been tested before. So this was a new learning experience.

Behind him there was a shout. A splash.

Finn spun and saw Leo struggling and gasping in

the reeds at the lake's edge. Kayla was a few steps farther away, but she ran toward Leo, the pastor right behind her.

Finn got there first, tromped into the mud and reeds, yanking his feet out of the sucking mud with each step. "I'm coming, buddy," he called, keeping his voice calm. "I've got you."

Everyone on the shore was shouting, the two little girls were screaming, but he blocked it all out and focused on Leo. He got his hands around the boy's torso and lifted, and was rewarded with a punch in the face.

He shook it off like you'd shake off a buzzing bee, ignored the boy's flailing and carried him toward shore. Once Leo realized he was safe, he started to cry in earnest and clung to Finn.

The feeling of a little boy in his arms, the relief of saving him, of not losing another kid on his watch, overwhelmed Finn and he hugged Leo right back. Then he put the boy into Kayla's arms.

She sank to the ground, holding and cuddling Leo. "You're okay, you're okay," she said, stroking his hair, using the edge of her sleeve to wipe mud and tears from his face.

He was okay. Praise God.

Kayla looked up at Finn. "Thank you."

He shook his head. "I should have been clear about the safety rules." He'd thought Willie was in charge of the trip and would have told them to stay away from that soggy edge, but apparently not, and he shouldn't rely on someone else. When would he learn that it was his responsibility to keep kids safe?

"That's not a way to end a fishing trip," Willie said.

"Let's take a lunch break. The two of you can grab some clean clothes and come back."

"I'll dry right off in the sun," Finn said. "Leo can change if he wants, and then I'd like to see if I could help him catch a fish."

For whatever reason, the boy was afraid of him, and for whatever reason, Finn seemed to want to stop that. So be it. It didn't have to mean anything.

"I'll dry off here, too," Leo said, straightening up and stepping away from Kayla. Trying to be a little man. Finn's throat tightened.

He was hunting around for a bobber in Willie's fishing box when he noticed a small laminated photo. "Who's this?" he asked.

Willie looked at the photo and shook his head. "My granddaughter who died."

Finn stared at the little blonde, obscured by cracked and yellowing laminate. "I didn't know. I'm sorry."

Willie shrugged. "I don't talk about it much, but there's not a day I don't think of her." He sighed. "You get used to it. Not over it, but used to it."

"I haven't."

Willie nodded. "It takes time."

Finn looked at the older man, always upbeat, always quick with a helping hand or a joke to cheer up other people. It was a good reminder: Finn wasn't the only person in the world who'd suffered a loss.

After they'd fished and each of the children had caught at least one, Kayla offered to take the kids to her cabin to get them cleaned up and give them a snack. "And you can meet our new dog," she said to the twins, earning squeals of delight.

Leo and the pastor's twins were getting to be friends.

That meant that Kayla and Carson would become friends, too; that was how it went when you were the parents of young children.

It made sense. But he didn't have to like it.

He didn't like the way the departing kids' laughter woke up his memories, either. Derek would have loved to fish and play with dogs. But thanks to Finn's own carelessness, he'd never get to do it.

Finn didn't deserve the kind of happiness that came to good people like the pastor and Kayla.

He roused himself from his reverie and started gathering the remaining gear to take back to his cabin. His leg ached, and he stopped to rub it.

"You're hurting today." Carson Blair knelt and picked up a few loose pieces of fishing gear.

"Yeah." Finn straightened. "Thought you'd be going up to Kayla's with your girls."

"She and Willie said they can handle them for a bit," Carson said. "I'll help you carry stuff up to the main house. It'll give me the chance to talk to you."

He was going to speak to Finn about Kayla. "No need," he said. "I'm fine."

"Are you sure about that?"

The man was annoying. "Yes, I'm sure."

"Well, I'm not," Carson said. "You've got some kind of issue with me, and I'd like to know what it is. I think we could work together, make good things happen, at church and in town and at this ranch, but not if you're mad about something I don't even understand."

The words burst out before Finn could stop them. "You need to leave my employees alone."

Carson raised an eyebrow. "Is that what Kayla is to you? An employee?"

"Yes, and she's got a job to do here. She doesn't need any distractions."

"Funny, she told me she was off today."

"You calling me out?" Finn's fists clenched.

Carson raised a hand like a stop sign. "I'm not calling you out. I'm a pastor. It's sort of against the rules." A slight smile quirked his face. "Besides which, I know my limits. I couldn't take you." He turned and started walking. "Come on. I'll help you carry this stuff up."

Finn hesitated and then fell into step beside the man. The momentary break gave him time to think. He didn't have any right to Kayla, and there was no good reason for him to be throwing his weight around, setting limits.

"Sorry," he said as he fell into step beside the pastor. "Didn't mean to act like a thug."

Carson chuckled. "You're hardly that." He paused. "But…if I might make a suggestion, have you considered talking to someone about your grief issues?"

Finn's ire rose again. "I've got my issues under control."

"Do you?" The pastor's question was mild, but his face showed skepticism. "You seem a little quick to anger. A lot of times, that's about something other than the issue at hand. Although," he added, "I can see why you'd be defensive of Kayla. She's a lovely woman."

Finn glowered.

"And I'm interested in a purely pastoral sense. I don't have time for anything more. But you—" he turned and faced Finn down "—you need to get yourself straight with God before you have anything to offer a good woman like Kayla."

Finn schooled his face for a sermon. And closed his mind against the tiny ray of hope that wanted in. Because getting himself straight with God wasn't going to happen, no matter what a flowers-and-sunshine pastor had to say.

On Monday morning, Kayla took her time strolling toward the kennel for her morning shift.

Magpies chattered and barn swallows skimmed the fields, low and graceful in the still-cool morning air. She lifted her face and sent up a prayer of thanks.

Leo had gone eagerly to camp this morning, none the worse for his tumble into the pond two days before. Just the memory of it sent a shudder through Kayla, but it was rapidly followed by more gratitude, this time for Finn.

He'd been instantly alert and had rescued Leo almost before Kayla had realized the gravity of the situation. Willie and Pastor Carson had rushed in to provide sympathy and comfort.

Having all that support had melted Kayla. She'd been raising Leo virtually alone since his birth. Mitch hadn't been a partner, but a threat to be wary about. And he'd cut her off from most of her old friends.

Kayla was independent; she'd had to be, growing up with her parents.

The sudden, warm feeling she'd gotten, that she and Leo were part of a caring community—that was something she treasured, something she felt a timid wish to build. She'd made a start yesterday at church, introducing herself to more people and signing up for a women's book discussion later in July.

She felt the urge to build something with Finn, too, but she wasn't willing to explore that. Neither, from the looks of things, was he.

He did give her a friendly wave when she walked into the kennel. "I'm putting the dogs from the first row out into the run. I'll supervise 'em if you clean?"

"Sure." She smiled at him. It was nice he'd phrased it as a question, when in reality he was the boss and could call the shots.

She started removing toys and beds and dishes from the kennels in preparation for hosing them down. The cleaning protocol they'd set up helped prevent disease, and it also made for a nice environment for the animals. For many, it was the best place they'd ever lived.

She opened the door to the last kennel on the end and saw something dark on the floor. Blood.

"Finn!" She left everything where it was and headed to the doorway. "I think that new dog, Winter, is sick." She scanned the field and located the big female, sitting watchful, away from the other dogs.

"What's going on?" Finn had been kneeling beside Axel, but now he stood and came over. "Is she acting different?"

"Take a look at her kennel. I'll watch the dogs."

He went inside and she knelt and called to Winter. She'd been dropped off the previous day by a couple of guys, neighbors of her owner. They'd rescued her from what they said was an abusive situation, but Finn, who'd talked with them, hadn't offered up any more details.

The dog looked over, ears hanging long, cloudy eyes mournful.

"Come here, girl," Kayla encouraged and felt in her pocket for a treat. She checked to make sure no aggressive dogs were nearby and then held it out to Winter.

The dog came closer, walking with a hunched, halting gait, but stopped short and cringed back as Finn emerged from the kennel. He held up his phone. "That was blood. I called the vet," he said. "Her new-dog appointment was supposed to be today, but he had to cancel. He says he can come out but he has to bring his baby boy."

She nodded, still watching the wary dog. "What do you think is wrong with Winter?"

Finn shook his head slowly, his mouth twisting. "The story is that she had a litter of stillborn pups. The owner got mad and started beating her."

Kayla gasped. "Who *does* that?" Sudden tears blurred her vision. The dog was beautiful, one of God's innocent creatures. That someone would feel he had the right to abuse her...

"The guys who dropped her off say they're going to call him up on animal abuse charges. But they wanted to make sure she was safe first." He studied the dog. "I'll step away. She's probably afraid of men, and for good reason. Maybe you can get her to come over."

It took continued encouragement and the tossing of several treats before the dog got close enough for Kayla to touch her.

"Be careful," Finn said quietly from his position on the other side of the dog run. "She's been treated badly. She may bite."

Kayla clicked her tongue and held out another treat, then carefully reached out to rub the dog's chest. Winter let out a low whine.

"Here, baby. Have a snack." She waved the remaining treat, gently.

The dog grabbed it from her hand and retreated to a safe distance to eat.

"You stay out here with her," Finn said. "I'll get

the rest of the kennels clean and then bring the other dogs in. I worry about contagion. No telling what she's picked up."

So Kayla sat in the sun, sweet-talking the old dog. After Finn took the other dogs in, as the day warmed up, Winter approached close enough that Kayla could scratch her ears.

She patted the ground. "Go ahead—relax. Just rest."

But the dog remained alert, jumping up when a chipmunk raced past, then sinking back down on her haunches, head on front paws, eyes wary.

Kayla knew how *that* felt. "It's hard to relax when you're worried for your safety, isn't it?" she crooned. "It's all right. We'll protect you here."

What was true for the dog might be true for Kayla, too. Sometimes, during the past week, she'd felt her habitual high-alert state ebb away. Even now, the hot sun melted tension from her shoulders.

After half an hour, she heard a vehicle approach and a door slam. Soon Finn appeared with a jeans-clad man he introduced as Dr. DeMoise.

"Call me Jack," the tall vet said easily, shifting a wide-eyed baby from one shoulder to the other so he could shake her hand.

"Your son's beautiful," Kayla said. Without her willing it, her arms reached for the baby boy. "Do you think he'll let me hold him?"

"Most likely." The vet smiled his thanks. "He's not real clingy yet."

She lifted the baby from his arms. The child— probably about six months old—stared at her with wide eyes and started to fuss a little. Kayla walked and hummed and clucked to him. Comforting a baby must be like riding a bike: it came back easily. Leo had been colicky, and she'd spent a lot of time soothing him.

Now, holding the vet's baby close and settling him, longing bloomed inside her. She hadn't let herself think about having another baby, not when she was with Mitch, and not in the difficult year after getting divorced, when she'd been struggling to start a business and fend him off. Now desire for another little one took her breath away.

Forget about it, she ordered herself.

But with Leo growing up so fast…

The baby stiffened and let out a fussy cry, probably sensing her inner conflict. She breathed in and out slowly and walked him around the field.

Once she'd gotten the baby calmed down, she watched as Jack squatted near the dog, who seemed to be in increasing distress. Finn leaned against the fence several feet away, watching.

"I'm wondering if she's got another pup," the vet said finally. "You said her litter was stillborn?"

"And her owner beat her right after she gave birth."

The vet grimaced. "I'm going to need to take her in, but let's see what she's trying to do now, first. Couple of clean towels?"

Finn went inside and the doctor examined the dog and pressed her abdomen gently.

Kayla walked over, swaying gently with the baby. "Is she going to be okay?"

The vet frowned. "I hope so. It's good you called."

"Could she have another live pup?"

"No. Not after almost a day, not likely." He rubbed the dog's ears, gently. "But we'll do our best to take care of Mama, here. She doesn't deserve what happened to her."

"Nobody does." Kayla leaned closer and saw a couple of wounds on the dog's back and leg.

Finn handed the towels to the doctor and then came over to stand by Kayla. He smiled at Jack's baby, reached out and tickled his leg, and the baby allowed it.

"This one's not afraid of you. Lots of babies are scared of men. At least…" At least, they'd been afraid of Mitch.

"Sammy's been raised by his dad for the last six months," Finn explained as they both watched the vet work with Winter. "He and his wife adopted him, but she passed away, so now he's a single dad."

"Awww." She swayed with the baby to keep him calm.

"Jack is the only vet within thirty miles, so he has a busy practice. When his wife died and he had to care for Sammy full-time… It's been rough."

"Day care?"

"He's got a part-time nanny, but apparently, she's not working out."

The vet rose and walked over to them. "I'll drive my van to the gate so we can get her into the clinic. If one of you wants to come along…"

"I can," Kayla said instantly. "I can take care of Sammy and help with the dog."

"No." Finn frowned. "I'll go."

"But—" She didn't want to let the baby out of her arms.

"I need you to finish up here," he said abruptly.

Jack gave them both a quizzical look. "Whatever you two decide. I'll be right back with the van. Just make sure the dog stays still."

After he'd left, Kayla spoke up. "I just thought, since I've got the baby calmed down—"

"I don't want you going into town with Jack. People will make something of it." His face was set.

Kayla pressed her lips together. It was almost as if Finn felt possessive of her. Which didn't make any sense.

But it *did* feel familiar, and scarily so. Mitch had started out just a little possessive, but that had expanded until he got outraged if she had a conversation with a male cashier or said "thank you" to a guy holding open a door for her.

Finn's attitude was probably about something else. There was no reason a man like Finn should have any feelings at all about her, possessive or otherwise.

But she needed to be careful, and stay alert, and not get too involved. Just in case Finn bore any similarity to Mitch.

Chapter Six

That Friday evening, Finn turned his truck into the road that led to Redemption Ranch with mixed feelings—mixed enough that he pulled over, telling himself he needed to check on Winter and her new foster puppy, crated in the back.

Truth was, he wanted to get his head together before he got back to the ranch.

The trip to pick up Winter from the vet clinic had been a welcome opportunity to escape from a work environment that had him in close proximity to Kayla for much of the day.

He opened the back of the pickup and checked on the two dogs. Winter lay still, but with her head upright and alert. The young pup beside her had been a surprise, but so right that Finn had quickly agreed to take both back to the ranch.

He took his time adjusting the crates and rubbing Winter's head through the side bars, aware that he was just procrastinating on returning to the ranch and Kayla. He wanted to stay uninvolved, but he couldn't seem to pull it off. When he'd seen Kayla holding that baby earlier in the week, he'd gotten gushy, romantic, old-movie feelings, until memories crashed in and washed them away in a sea of cold guilt. And then, just to top off his own ridiculousness, he'd gone caveman on her, refusing to allow her to go help Jack. Which was just plain stupid. Jack was single, and eligible, and deserving of happiness, and why *wouldn't* he like Kayla, especially when she'd shown such tenderness toward his son?

But before he'd had the sense to think that through, he'd gotten in Jack's face, insisting that Kayla couldn't go into town with Winter, that he, Finn, had to be the one to go himself.

What was wrong with Finn, that he was acting like a Neanderthal around this woman whose personal life was absolutely none of his business?

Possessive stuff. No matter what his brain said, his emotions wanted to mark her as his.

It was almost like he wanted to be a husband and father again.

Finn pushed the thoughts away by turning up the country music louder. And then was rewarded with songs about hurting love. He released a huff and started the truck again.

He pulled up toward the kennel and tried not to look to the right, at Kayla's place. But there were Penny and Willie, carrying a table from the next cabin down the road and into the yard in front of Kayla's porch. He rolled down a window to see what was going on, and the smell of grilling meat sent his stomach rumbling.

"Come on—join in," Willie called, beckoning with his free arm.

What could he do but pull over and stop the truck? The cessation of movement started Winter barking, so he had to get her out of the crate. And then the pup cried, so he had to be brought out, too.

And that brought everyone running over to see.

Finn knelt beside Winter and the fragile pup, trying to help them get their bearings. Trying to get his own, as well.

Leo shouted and reached out, and the puppy cringed.

"Careful!" Finn said.

Only when Leo shrank back did Finn realize he'd boomed out the word too loudly.

"You left with one and came back with two?" Penny asked, kneeling to see the dogs and, not coincidentally, putting herself at Leo's height. She put a hand on the kid's shoulder. "That's not her pup, is it?"

"It is now." Finn couldn't help but smile as the puppy yapped up at Winter and she gave him a chastening slurp of her tongue, knocking him into his place. Quickly, he explained how the unlikely pairing had come to pass.

Willie was setting up horseshoes, and Long John sat in a chair, shucking corn. "Looks like a party," Finn said, loud enough for the two older veterans to hear.

"Cooking out. It's Friday." Willlie grinned. "Not that I've worked that hard all week, but habit is habit."

"Do you need a blanket for the dogs to rest on?" It was Kayla's husky voice, and when he turned toward her, he saw that she already had one in hand. Of course, she'd seen the need and filled it, quietly and efficiently. That was who she was.

They settled the dogs off to the side of the picnic table. "Why is there a pup, Mom?" Leo asked, pressing against Kayla's side. "You said she had babies that died."

"I don't know. Ask Mr. Gallagher."

But Leo pressed his lips together and stayed tight by Kayla's side.

Great. Finn had managed to spook the poor kid. "Winter wasn't feeling well after her puppies didn't make it," he said, simplifying and cleaning it up for young ears. "And Dr. Jack had a pup at the clinic who didn't have a mom."

"The Good Lord has a way of working things out," Willie said. "Joy out of sorrow." He gave Finn a meaningful look.

Finn's jaw tightened, because he knew what Willie was thinking. That Finn was supposed to find some kind of redemption out of the loss he'd faced.

It wasn't happening. Not now, not ever.

"This corn's ready to throw on the grill," Long John called.

"Chicken's almost done," Penny said.

"Ooh, I've got to check on my apple cobbler." Kayla hurried inside.

Willie came over to where Finn stood. "You as hungry as I am?"

Finn noticed Leo watching them. On an impulse, he clutched his hands across his abdomen and fake-fell to the ground. "Starving!" he groaned.

Willie laughed and nudged Finn with his boot. "Get up, boy. Them that don't work, don't eat."

Finn jumped to his feet. By now, Leo was smiling, just a little. "I'll do anything," Finn said, "for apple cobbler."

"Then get inside and help her carry out the dishes, and make it snappy." Willie rolled his eyes at Leo. "Think I'll ever be able to make this big lug behave?"

Leo laughed outright. "He's a grown-up! He doesn't have to behave."

"That's where you're wrong," Willie said. "Grown-ups have to behave even better than kids. Right, Finn?"

"I'm going, I'm going." He glanced over at Leo, who was still smiling. "Keep an eye on those dogs for me, will you?"

"Yeah!" Leo hurried in their direction. Finn waited just long enough to see that the boy knelt carefully, not getting too close.

"I'll keep an eye, too," Willie murmured to Finn. "Now, I'm serious. If you want dinner, you'd better help the lady get it on the table."

Finn reached Kayla's small kitchen just in time to see her lift the cobbler out of the oven. Her cheeks were pink and her eyes bright, and he wondered how he'd ever thought her plain.

She met his eyes, and it seemed to him her color heightened. "I... Dinner's almost ready. I hope you'll join us."

"I'd like to." His playful mood from trying to jolly Leo up lingered, and he assumed a hangdog look. "But Willie told me I can't unless I do my share of the work. Give me a job?"

She chuckled, and the sound ran along his nerve endings. "There's never a shortage. You can carry out the plates and silverware. Then come back, and I'll have more for you to do."

"Yes, ma'am." He inhaled. "That smells fantastic."

"I have some talents."

"I can see that."

Their eyes locked for a moment, and Finn was sure he detected some sort of interest, not just casual, in hers. His own chest almost hurt with wanting to get closer to this woman. And he could barely remember why he'd thought that was a bad idea.

She turned away from him, laughing a little. "Go on. Get to work."

So he carried out the flatware and plates, and then went back for several more loads. Penny called him into action to help at the grill, and then Willie remembered there was a fresh pitcher of lemonade down at his cabin. Long John offered to get it, going so far as to stand up, but Finn waved off the offer and walked down to get it. Limp or no, he was still more able-bodied than Long John.

It felt like a party, but more than that, it felt like family. And Finn, whose relatives all lived back East, hadn't had that sense in years.

Two years, to be specific. Since Deirdre and Derek had died.

But for the first time in a long time, that thought didn't send him into darkness. He set it aside, because he wanted to focus on the here and now, just for a little bit longer.

So they ate their fill of grilled chicken and corn on the cob, Long John's famous coleslaw, and potato salad Penny had picked up from the deli in town. She'd gotten ice cream, too, so when the main meal was over, there was that for the cobbler.

The dogs, Winter and the new pup as well as Shoney, went up and down the long table, begging. Finn couldn't be sure, but he suspected that all the dogs had gotten a few scraps. Himself, he'd concentrated on sneaking food to Shoney, who couldn't see the many crumbs and pieces that dropped to the ground.

Finally, they'd all eaten their fill, and more. Leo asked to be excused and was soon rolling on the ground with the dogs. Penny started clearing dishes. When Finn stood to help, she waved him away. "Take it easy for a bit," she said. "The kitchen's only big enough for one. You, too, Kayla. Sit back and relax."

"No, I'll wash and you can dry," Kayla compromised.

"Seems to me," Willie said, his eyes twinkling, "that a boy of Leo's age might like to play a little Frisbee or catch. But my old bones ache too much to do a game justice." He looked at Finn. "How about you?"

Finn hadn't missed how Leo's eyes lit up. "It'd be good to work off some of this fine food," he said and glanced up at Kayla. "Okay with you?"

"Of course, if he wants to." She turned toward Leo and then shrugged. "Just ask him."

It was tacit permission for Finn to form his own relationship with Leo. And while he knew it wasn't a good idea long-term, some lazy, relaxed, happy part of himself couldn't worry about that just now.

"Think I've got a couple of mitts and a softball down in my storage cupboard," Willie said and started to get up.

"I'll get it if you tell me where." This time, Finn took his cane, wanting to save his leg for the actual game of catch.

And that was how Finn ended up teaching Leo how to throw like a pitcher and how to hold his mitt, while Willie and Long John relaxed in lawn chairs and offered advice.

It felt like an unexpected blessing. Leo, who seemed at times timid as a mouse, was smiling and laughing and, to all appearances, enjoying himself enough that he didn't seem to want to stop.

Out here, tossing a softball back and forth as the sun sank behind the Sangre de Cristos, it was easy for Finn to focus on what was good in his life. This work that benefited other creatures, both human and canine, in a concrete way. This place, with its open spaces and views of the jagged mountain range that seemed to point the way directly to heaven. These people, who'd struggled enough in their lives to understand others rather than judge them.

Back in Virginia, after everything had gone so terribly wrong, he'd sunk too deep into himself, to where he could only see what was bad and wrong inside him. It was the kind of shame and guilt that threatened to make you want to do away with yourself, and although it would have been deserved, and he'd come close, some faint inner light had told him it was wrong. He'd dragged himself to church and talked to the pastor, older than Finn and wiser, about getting a fresh start. He was suffocating in Virginia, and all he'd felt the smallest shred of desire for was the open spaces of the West, where he'd sometimes traveled for work. Next thing, the pastor had been calling his old high school friend, Penny. The job had fallen into place so neatly that Finn, who didn't normally put much stock in God reaching down from the sky and fixing things, felt there'd been some of that going on.

Maybe Kayla and Leo's arrival had been a God thing, too.

Finally, he felt the chill in the darkening air and realized that Leo was yawning, and wondered aloud whether it was time to go inside.

"Not when there's a fire to be built." Willie got up and dragged an old fire-pit bowl from the back of the house. "Hey, Leo, can you give me a hand picking up sticks?"

"And I'll get the logs," Finn said with a mock sigh.

As they taught Leo how to build a fire—with appropriate safety warnings—Finn had a reluctant realization.

He hadn't wanted to get involved with people, especially women and kids. He'd come to Redemption Ranch to focus on making retribution, giving something back to a world from which he'd taken so much away. To lose himself amid the mountains that made even a hulk like him feel small. Not to grow close to a pair of souls who tugged at him, made his heart want to come alive again.

But want to or not, it had happened.

Kayla washed the last dish and handed it to Penny, then let the water out of the sink. "Thanks for helping," she said. "We got done in half the time."

"Yes, we did." Penny hung the pan on the overhead hook.

"No thanks to you," she scolded Shoney, who'd been roaming the kitchen and generally getting underfoot, looking for dropped food and occasionally finding it. Kayla dried her hands, knelt to rub the dog's shaggy head, and then stood and headed for the door. "I'd better go see how Leo's doing."

"He's doing fine." Penny put a hand on Kayla's arm, stopping her. "I can see him out the window. He's with Willie and Finn."

"And he's not acting scared of Finn?"

"Come see." Penny gestured out the window.

Kayla looked and sucked in a breath.

In the background, the setting sun made rosy fire on the mountains. Swallows skimmed and swooped, catching insects for an evening snack, chirring and squeaking their pleasure. The dogs sprawled on the blanket she'd brought out, the new puppy spooned in close to Winter.

And there was Leo, laughing up at something Willie had said, while Finn looked on fondly.

They weren't related by blood, but they were interacting like three generations. It was what she'd always wanted for Leo.

"Does he have a grandpa?" Penny asked.

Kayla shook her head. "His father's parents have both passed, and my dad…"

Penny was wiping off the counter, but at Kayla's pause she stopped and looked at her.

"My dad's in prison for life." She said it all in a rush, as she did every time she had to discuss her dad with anyone. Then she knelt and pulled Shoney against her, rubbing the shaggy head.

"That's rough." Penny leaned back against the counter, her face sympathetic rather than judgmental. "Did that happen when you were a kid, or later?"

"When I was twelve." She'd remember the day forever, even though she'd tried to push it out of her mind. Coming home from school to police cars every which way in the front yard. The neighbors whispering and gawking. And then her father, coming out of the house, swearing and fighting the two officers who were trying to control him.

It had been another couple of years before she'd gotten her mother to tell her the charge. "He shot a convenience-store clerk," she said now to Penny. "A robbery gone bad. Drugs." She looked at the floor. "The man he killed was the father of three kids. And he disabled a police officer trying to escape."

"Oh, honey." Penny held out her arms, and when Kayla

didn't stand to walk into them, she came right over and wrapped her arms around Kayla and Shoney both. "That must have been so hard."

Kayla felt a little pressure behind her eyes, but she had no intention of crying. She cleared her throat and took a step back. "It *was* hard. Kids can be cruel."

"Did you have brothers and sisters?"

"Nope. Just me. I was a mistake."

Penny stared and slowly began shaking her head back and forth. "Oh, no. No, you weren't. God doesn't make mistakes."

Kayla waved a hand. "I know. I know. It's fine. It's just…that's how my parents looked at it, is all."

"You ever talk to anyone about that?" Penny asked.

Kayla's eyebrows came together. "I'm talking to you."

"I mean a therapist."

"No. No way." Her dad's issues, and her mom's problems after the arrest, were part of a big box of heartache she didn't want to open.

"So your parents had issues, let you know they hadn't planned to have you." Penny lifted an eyebrow. "How old were you when you married the abuser?"

Kayla's jaw about dropped. "What? What does that have to do with my folks?"

Penny took the dish towel from Kayla's hands, folded it once and hung it on the stove handle. "I just think it's interesting that you chose a man who didn't value you properly, after being with parents who maybe did the same. Patterns." Penny looked out the window. "We repeat patterns."

The older woman's words hit too close to home. After her father had gone to prison, Kayla had tried to stay close to her mother, as close as the multiple boyfriends and stepfathers would permit. But when her mom had been killed in a drinking-related car accident...yeah. Kayla had connected with Mitch almost immediately, drawn to his self-assurance and dominant personality.

Kayla didn't want to think about what that all might mean, psychologically. Instead, she turned the tables. "Are you speaking from experience?"

"Touché," Penny said. "I sure am. And one day, you and I can sit down and talk about it, maybe. All I know is, I'm not quick to put my trust in any man. But it's important to trust someone. I want you to know you can trust me."

"Why?" Kayla asked bluntly. She didn't understand why Penny was being intrusive, and she *really* didn't understand why she was being kind.

"I've watched how you interact with your son for a couple of weeks now. You're a good mom." Penny smiled at her. "And more relevant to me, you're a good worker. I'd like to keep you around."

A sudden thickness settled in Kayla's throat. "Thanks."

"And when I said what I did about men, I wasn't talking about Finn. He's one of the good ones. So are Long John and Willie, for that matter."

Kayla nodded but didn't speak. Penny might think these men were good, and trustworthy, and probably on some level they were. But on the flip side, they were military men and loyal to their band of brothers.

Men like Mitch.

"We're done in here," she said instead of answering. "Want to go outside by the fire?"

"For a bit, sure." Penny's eyes were hooded, and Kayla was suddenly sorry she hadn't pursued Penny's remarks about men. She got the feeling that the older woman had a story that was plenty interesting, not to mention a few issues of her own.

She led the way, but when she got to where she could see the fire, she stopped. Penny almost ran into her.

Willie was playing guitar, softly, and Long John picked harmony on his banjo. The fire burned low, sending the warm, friendly smell of wood smoke in their direction.

And Leo was sleeping in Finn's arms.

Kayla drew in a deep breath and let it out slowly. There was something about a man who was good with kids. Something about a man big enough to hold a five-year-old boy with no problem, and confident enough in his masculinity to be nurturing.

Penny walked past and perched on a log beside Willie. They spoke for a moment, low, and then Willie launched into another song, a love song Kayla remembered from when she was a kid.

Penny stared into the fire, a remote expression on her face.

Kayla walked over to Finn's side. "Are you okay holding him?" she asked. "He can get heavy."

"It's not a problem." But his face was serious, his eyes a little…sad? Troubled?

So they all sat around for a little while longer, huddling in the warmth of the fire. A circle of humans in the light of the moon, seeking warmth, needing each other.

In the distance, there was a howl.

"What's that?" she asked.

"Coyote," Long John said. "Keep the dogs and the boy near home tonight."

Kayla shivered and scooted her log a little closer to the fire's warmth.

She looked around at the faces, old and young. She'd

gotten almost close to these people in the past two weeks, and she never got close. She liked being here, liked being with them.

She especially liked being with Finn, if she were honest with herself. They'd fallen into an easy routine, working together in the kennels, sharing information about the dogs and the weather and the ranch. They laughed at the same jokes on the country-music station, liked the same songs. Both of them usually carried a book around for slow moments, and he'd turned her on to Louis L'Amour.

All the connections were something to enjoy, but also something to be cautious about. She'd liked being around Mitch and his friends at first, too.

Of course, looking back at it, she couldn't miss the warning signs. Why had she chosen Mitch?

There was the obvious fact that no one else had wanted her. And that she'd wanted to have a baby like nobody's business. Still, she should have had more sense.

Unless Penny was right, and it had to do with her parents, her childhood.

Willie played a last riff on his guitar and then looked over at Long John, who'd fallen silent. "That's it for me," he said. "These old bones are ready for bed, early as it is."

"It's not early when you get up for chores." Penny arched her back and stretched.

Both of the older men watched her, identical longing expressions on each weathered face.

Oh. So it was that way. And yet the two were best of friends, and Penny seemed oblivious to the way they'd been looking at her.

As they put their instruments away, Penny stood. "Thanks, everyone. See you tomorrow."

Willie cleared his throat. "Walk you home?"

Penny paused a beat. "No. Thanks, but I'm fine." She turned and headed for the road at a good clip.

"Can't blame a guy for trying," Willie muttered.

Long John gave him a look. "She's the same age as your daughter." He started to heave himself up out of his chair, then sank back with a sigh.

Willie held out a hand, and Long John hesitated, then grasped it and got to his feet. Willie picked up both musical instruments, and the two of them headed back toward their cabins.

That left Kayla alone with Finn, who still held the sleeping Leo in his arms. "I...I'll put out the fire." She felt absurdly uncomfortable.

He nodded. His face was hard to read. Was he enjoying holding Leo or was it a burden for him?

His face suggested something else entirely, but she wasn't sure what.

Finn watched as Kayla hauled a bucket of water to the metal fire pit. She was tiny, but she lifted the heavy bucket easily and poured it on.

That was Kayla—however vulnerable she appeared on the outside, there was solid strength hidden beneath.

She straightened and put her hands to the small of her back. "I should probably bring another bucket of water, right?"

"Just to be sure. I'm sorry I can't help you."

"You're helping, believe me." She gave her sleeping child a tender glance before taking the bucket back over to the outside spigot.

Finn felt the weight of the five-year-old boy against him as if it were lead. Pressing him down into the lawn chair.

Pressing him into his past.

He'd held his own son just like this. It was such a sweet age, still small enough to fit into a lap and to want to be there.

Leo would soon grow beyond such tenderness.

Derek wouldn't, not ever.

The knowledge of that ached in Finn's chest. Outside of the guilt and the regret, he just plain missed his son.

Would Derek have been shy and quiet, like Leo? Or more blustery and outgoing like his cousins, kids Finn never saw anymore because he couldn't stand his brothers' sympathy?

Kayla sloshed another bucket over the fire pit. "There. No sparks left to cause a fire."

He met her eyes and the thought flashed through him: *there are still some sparks here, just not the fire-pit kind.*

But although it was true, it wouldn't do to highlight the fact. "Do you want me to carry him inside?"

She hesitated, and he could understand why. It was an intimate thing to do. Yet a sleeping five-year-old was substantial, and he could bear the burden more easily than she could. Despite the ache in his leg, he wanted to play the man's role rather than watching a small, slight woman do all the heavy lifting.

Before she could refuse him, he stood, carefully holding Leo's head against his shoulder. The boy stirred a little, then cuddled marginally tighter and relaxed against Finn.

His throat too tight to say anything, he inclined his head, inviting Kayla to lead the way inside.

It was tricky, but he used his free hand and good leg

to climb the ladder to the sleeping loft, following behind Kayla. He had to duck his head beneath the slanted roof. When he went to put Leo down, his leg went out from under him and he lurched, making Kayla gasp. But he caught himself and managed to place the boy carefully on his low, narrow cot, made up with faded race-car sheets.

The sight of those sheets hurt his heart a little. Kayla must have packed them up and brought them along, wanting to give her child a taste of home. "Sorry about that," he said, gesturing at his leg. "I wouldn't drop him."

"No, it's fine, thank you! I forgot that climbing might be hard for you."

He shrugged. "My pleasure."

"I guess he's finally used to you," she said as she pulled the sheets and blankets up to cover Leo's narrow shoulders.

"It took some doing, but yeah."

"He...he's seen some scary things. His father...well."

"Same man that gave you the bruises?" he asked mildly.

Her sharp intake of breath wasn't unexpected, but Finn was tired of the distance between them, the concealment, the connections that weren't getting made. Something about this night made him want to throw caution away and nudge her a little, see if the thing he felt was there for her, too.

She ran a hand over Leo's hair, not looking at Finn. "Yes," she said, her voice so low he had to bend closer to hear it. "Same guy."

"If I could get my hands on him, I'd be tempted to do worse to him than he did to you and Leo." Because the words were confrontational, he kept his tone mild.

She glanced up at him, secrets in her eyes. And then she rose, gracefully, to her feet. "It's late."

Yes, it was, and he didn't want to go. He climbed the ladder down ahead of her, so he could catch her if she fell—odd protective urge, since she was probably up and down the ladder a dozen times a day. At the bottom, he waited.

She stepped off the last rung. The slow way she turned, he could tell she knew he was there, close. "Finn…"

He reached out for her, touched her chin. "You're a good mother and a good cook," he said. "Thank you for tonight."

That was all he meant to do; just thank her. But the unexpectedly soft feel of her skin made his hand linger, and then splay to encompass her strong jawline, her soft hair.

She looked up at him through long, thick lashes. There was a light spray of freckles across her nose.

Finn's heart swelled with tenderness, and he lowered his face toward hers.

Chapter Seven

Kayla drew in a panicky breath and reached out, feeling the rough stubble of Finn's face. He was going to kiss her and she wanted him to.

But he stopped short and brushed her cheek with his finger. "Your skin is so soft. I didn't shave. I'm afraid I'll hurt you."

She inhaled the piney, outdoorsy scent of him and her heart thudded, heavy and hard. "You won't hurt me," she whispered.

He narrowed his eyes just a tiny bit, studying her, as if to test her sincerity.

And then he pulled her closer and lowered his lips the rest of the way down to hers.

Tenderness and respect? She'd never experienced kissing this way. It made her want to pull him closer, but she didn't dare. And after a moment, he lifted up to look at her. "You're like a tiny little sparrow, ready to fly away."

His whimsical description amused her, cutting through the moment's intensity. "Sometimes I've wished I could fly," she admitted, her voice still soft, heart still pounding.

Dear Reader,

IT'S A FACT: if you answer 4 quick questions, we'll send you **4 FREE REWARDS!**

I'm not kidding you. As a leading publisher of women's fiction, we value your opinions… and your time. That's why we are prepared to **reward** you handsomely for completing our mini-survey. In fact, we have 4 Free Rewards for you, including 2 free books and 2 free gifts.

As you may have guessed, that's why our mini-survey is called **"4 for 4".** Answer 4 questions and get 4 Free Rewards. It's that simple!

Thank you for participating in our survey,

Pam Powers

To get your 4 FREE REWARDS:
Complete the survey below and return the insert today to receive 2 FREE BOOKS and 2 FREE GIFTS guaranteed!

"4 for 4" MINI-SURVEY

1 Is reading one of your favorite hobbies?
☐ YES ☐ NO

2 Do you prefer to read instead of watch TV?
☐ YES ☐ NO

3 Do you read newspapers and magazines?
☐ YES ☐ NO

4 Do you enjoy trying new book series with FREE BOOKS?
☐ YES ☐ NO

YES! I have completed the above Mini-Survey. Please send me my 4 FREE REWARDS (worth over $20 retail). I understand that I am under no obligation to buy anything, as explained on the back of this card.

☐ I prefer the regular-print edition
105/305 IDL GMYL

☐ I prefer the larger-print edition
122/322 IDL GMYL

FIRST NAME	LAST NAME

ADDRESS

APT.#	CITY

STATE/PROV.	ZIP/POSTAL CODE

DETACH AND MAIL CARD TODAY!

® and ™ are trademarks owned and used by the trademark owner and/or its licensee. Printed in the U.S.A.

READER SERVICE—Here's how it works:

BUSINESS REPLY MAIL
FIRST-CLASS MAIL   PERMIT NO. 717   BUFFALO, NY

POSTAGE WILL BE PAID BY ADDRESSEE

READER SERVICE
PO BOX 1341
BUFFALO NY 14240-8571

NO POSTAGE
NECESSARY
IF MAILED
IN THE
UNITED STATES

"You did fly. You flew here to Redemption Ranch."

Yes, she had. She'd been flying away from something, someone.

From Mitch.

Reluctantly, she stepped back from the warm circle of Finn's arms. She looked at the floor across the room, embarrassed to meet his eyes, because she'd not only enjoyed his kiss, she'd returned it.

"Someday," he said, "I want to hear more about what you flew away from."

She bit her lip. She was starting to trust him, kind of wanted to tell him. Finn's solid protection and support would be such a blessing to her and Leo.

But there, as he crossed his arms and looked at her, was his Eighty-second Airborne tattoo. She still didn't know how attached he was to his unit, how close the bonds of brotherhood went for him.

Just because of who he was, she'd suspect the ties held tight. He was the loyal type, for sure. "The past isn't important," she said, not looking at him.

Something flashed in his eyes, some emotion. "I'm not sure I agree with you. If you don't deal with the past, you can't move forward."

"Moving forward is maybe overrated."

"Like us kissing?"

She huffed out a fake kind of laugh. "Yeah."

He cocked his head to one side, looking at her, his expression a little puzzled. "I don't understand women very well," he said. "And it's late. I should be going."

Something inside her wanted to cling on, to cry out, *No, don't go!* But that was the needy part of her that her mom had despised. The part that had experienced

Mitch's attention and glommed right on. "See you to-morrow," she said, forcing her voice to sound casual.

"Actually, not much," he said. "After the meeting to-morrow morning, I'll be away for the weekend."

"Oh." Her heart did a little plummet, and that was bad. She was already too attached, expecting to see him every day.

He must have heard something in her voice. "It's a reunion," he said, indicating his tattoo. "Eighty-second Airborne."

Her heart hit the floor. "Oh."

He laughed a little. "Bunch of old guys telling stories, mostly. But I love 'em. They're my brothers."

Of course they were. He'd do anything for his brothers.

Including, if it came to that, helping one of them find the woman who'd betrayed him and taken away his son. "Finn, about…this," she said, waving a hand, her cheeks heating. "We shouldn't… I mean, I don't—"

His face hardened. "I understand. We got carried away."

"Exactly. I just didn't want you to think…"

"That it meant something?"

It meant everything. "Exactly," she lied.

"Agreed," he said, his bearing going a little more upright and military. "See you."

And he was gone. The little lost girl inside Kayla curled up in a ball and cried at the loss of him.

She was hiding something.

Finn headed toward Penny's place for the dreaded semiannual meeting with the ranch's finance guy. Bingo, his current dog, loped along beside him.

"You have to act nice if you're coming to the meeting," Finn grumbled to the dog, but Bingo only laughed up at him. "I know. Penny will give you treats to make you behave."

The dog's tail started to wag at the *T* word.

Finn tried to focus on the dog, on the fresh morning air, on anything but the fact that he'd kissed Kayla last night. And she'd responded. She'd liked it.

And then she'd backed right off.

Had she heard the truth about Finn, or remembered it? Was that why she'd pushed him away?

But it wasn't just that. She was secretive, and he wanted to know why. Wanted to know what it was in her past that had her running. If they were going to be involved, he needed to know.

Were they going to be involved?

Probably not. For sure not. He'd made the decision, after losing his wife and son, that he wasn't going to go there again. Up until now, his grief had been so thick and dark that the promise hadn't been hard to keep.

But Kayla and Leo had made their way through his darkness and were battering at the hard shell surrounding his heart. He'd held Leo last night, held him for at least an hour, and the experience had softened something inside him.

Leo needed a father figure. And some part of Finn, apparently, needed a son.

But he didn't deserve a son. He didn't deserve to look forward, with hope, to the kind of happy new life that Derek and Deirdre would never have.

It was just that holding Kayla, kissing her, had been so very, very sweet. It had brought something inside him back to life.

He reached the main house. A glance at his phone told him he was early, so he settled on the edge of the porch.

If he *did* get involved with Kayla—and he wasn't saying he would, but if it happened—he wanted to know the truth about her. And, he rationalized, she was his employee. He needed to know.

Raakib Khan had served with Finn in the Eighty-second, and they'd had each other's backs. When Raakib came home, he'd started a little detective agency.

Finn called Raakib, shot the breeze for a minute and then gave him everything he knew about Kayla.

"What is your interest, my friend?" Raakib asked.

"She works for me."

"And is that all?"

Finn let out a disgusted snort. After all they'd been through together, Raakib could read him like a book. "That's all you need to know about," he growled and ended the call.

When he looked up, he saw Kayla walking toward him. His face heated. What had she heard?

She gave him a little wave and walked up the stairs toward the conference room. He got to his feet and followed, the dog ambling behind him.

Penny was in the kitchen, putting doughnuts on a tray, so he veered over her way. "You still sure about having Bingo here?"

"I think it's fine. It keeps us all in a good mood and reminds us of our mission."

He leaned closer. "Why is Kayla here?"

Penny shrugged. "I feel like we need all the ideas we can get. We're in trouble, Finn."

"Worse than I know?"

"You'll hear." She handed him the tray of doughnuts. "Carry this in there, will you? I'll be right in."

Their banker was there. A vet out of the Baltic, but you wouldn't have known it from his suit and dress shoes. Well, he was navy, after all.

He seemed to be grilling Kayla.

Finn wanted to protect her, felt that urge, except that she was holding her own. "No, I've never worked for this exact type of organization before," she admitted to Branson Howe. "But I volunteered with a nonprofit for kids, and I've run a business, so Penny thought I might be able to help. With the website or something."

She'd run a business? That was news to him.

Branson was frowning, arms crossed.

"We can use an outsider perspective," Finn said. "It's been just me and Penny since…well, since everything went haywire." He glanced over at Penny, who'd just walked in. Sometimes he worried about how she was dealing, or not dealing, with what had happened.

"It's okay, Finn—you can talk about it." Penny's abrupt tone called her words into question. "Coffee, everyone? We should get started."

"That's what I've been trying to do." Branson glared at Penny.

Undercurrents. You had to love them. Penny and Branson always circled around each other like two dogs getting ready to fight.

"You called the meeting," she said, "so why don't you tell us what's on your mind?"

Finn glanced at Kayla, who lifted an eyebrow back at him, obviously reading the back-and-forth as personal, the way he was. "I'll get you a cup of coffee," she offered. "Penny, do you need a refill?"

She waved a hand, leaning forward to look at Branson. "What's going on?"

"I just got a notice from the IRS." Branson opened his laptop and accepted a cup of coffee. "We missed a payment, and there's going to be a fine attached to it when we make it. We need to get on it and pay so the IRS doesn't flag us as suspicious. If that happens, we'll be in line for a lot of paperwork and audits."

"I thought the taxes, at least, were fine." Penny frowned. "We had an outside firm do them. They said they'd found enough deductions that we didn't have to pay anything."

Branson dropped his head and looked at her. "And you didn't question that?"

"No. I did pay them, of course... Oh." Penny smacked her forehead. "I'm an idiot."

"What?" Finn had to ask.

"I was going to get someone new for this year, but with as busy as I've been, I didn't. The outside firm was the one Harry chose, and I wonder..." She trailed off. "Again. I'm an idiot."

Harry. Penny's ex, and a poor excuse for a man.

"I looked into your tax people." Branson hesitated and looked at Penny. For the first time, a hint of sympathy twisted the corner of his mouth.

"I'm not made of glass. Give it to me straight."

"Apparently, one of the silent owners of your outside firm was Oneida Emerson. That could be why no forms were filed."

"None?" Penny's voice was casual, but her fists made red spots on her arms.

Again, Branson's eyes portrayed a little sympathy. "I'm hoping this is the last bad news I have to give you, from this situation, but I can't promise that," he said.

"Give it to me straight," Penny said. "Do you think we're going to make it? Or do we give up and shut down?"

"The vets and the dogs need us," Finn protested.

As if understanding his safe haven was at stake, Bingo let out a low whine and rested his head on Finn's knee.

"What about the grant we…you…just got?" Kayla asked.

"Can't be used for anything other than what we applied for. Improvements to the physical facility." Even if what they needed most was money for something else.

"What's the fine and back taxes likely to add up to?" Penny asked.

Branson named a number that was twice their operating budget.

Finn groaned and looked over at Penny. She was shaking her head. "If I could get my hands on Harry and his—" She bit off whatever she'd been going to say, but Finn could guess at it.

Even Bingo sighed and flopped to the floor, looking mournful.

"If you could just get some publicity and success stories out there, you might be able to raise enough in donations," Branson said. "You've barely started fundraising. But—"

"That's right," Kayla interrupted. "Everyone wants to support vets, and who can resist the dogs?"

"But we have no money for publicity, is the problem," Penny said. "No time to put together a campaign, either."

"Can't get water from a stone." Branson closed his

folder. "And neither of you has any background at fund-raising."

"You can't give up." Kayla leaned forward and looked in turn at everyone at the table. "Even if you don't have money, there are ways to get the word out."

Finn's heart squeezed as he looked at her earnest expression. It was sweet that she cared, given the short length of time she'd been here.

"I'm listening," Penny said in a dismissive tone that suggested she wasn't.

"Social media, for one. An updated website, for another."

"We have that stuff. It hasn't helped so far."

"Pardon me for saying so," Kayla said, "but it's all out of date. You—we, I'll help—need to keep that fresh and add new content."

"I know you're right," Penny said, "but I'm not posting pictures of the veterans. That's stood in our way."

"Well, okay, not without permission. But aren't there some who will ham it up for the camera? I'm sure Willie would."

Penny snorted out a laugh. "You're right about that."

"Capitalize on the setting. How warmhearted the community is." She sat up straighter, her cheeks flushing a little. "Maybe have an event that brings the whole community up here. And then photograph and video bits of it to use all year."

"It's a good idea," Penny said, "but wouldn't donations just trickle in? If Branson's right, we need money now."

"A fund-raising event isn't likely to bring in enough to weather this crisis, even if you could really get the word out," Branson said. "And what about when the next crisis comes?"

Finn debated briefly whether to speak up. But Kayla had changed the tone of the meeting and it had made him think of an idea that had been nudging at him. "Let me throw something out there," he said. "That old bunkhouse. If we renovated it, we might be able to host people to come up here."

"A working-ranch type of thing?" Penny looked skeptical. "That would take a lot of time, and our staff is small."

"But it's a possibility," Kayla said.

Penny frowned. "Wouldn't we have to have more ranch-type activities? Like riding horses and roping cattle or something?"

Finn snorted. "Not many ranches run according to that model anymore," he said.

"But," Penny said, "that's what people expect at a dude ranch. My sister worked at one for a while, and the Easterners want all the stereotypes."

Branson was shaking his head. "I don't like the liability issues, if you're having people do actual ranch work."

Kayla looked thoughtful. "I think people would enjoy coming out here for the peace." She waved a hand at the window. "Lots of people just want to get away. Relax. Reflect. This is a great place to do all that."

"This is getting to be pretty pie-in-the-sky," Branson said. "We need to pay our bills. You're talking about a renovation, lots of initial investment. You can't afford that."

"We have to start somewhere, Branson," Penny said impatiently. "Kayla and Finn are just suggesting some ideas. Which is more than I hear you doing."

Finn looked at Penny. She wasn't usually confrontational. He couldn't blame her, given that her husband

and his girlfriend had absconded with the ranch's funds. But she shouldn't take it out on Branson, who was, after all, a volunteer.

A volunteer who had a thing for Penny, if Finn's instincts were firing right.

Kayla snapped her fingers. "Crowdfunding. The kids' organization I volunteered for did it."

"I don't like it." Branson shook his head. "My niece tried to crowdfund to pay off her college loans, and then got mad when everyone in the extended family didn't donate."

"But this is a real cause," Penny said. "We're not just trying to avoid our responsibilities. Anyone who knows us knows how hard we work."

"*Do* they know, though?" Kayla asked. "Maybe we should do an open house *and* crowdfunding. People in the community could come up and see what we do, see the dogs and whatever vets are willing. We could talk about our mission. If we put that together with an online campaign, we might at least get some breathing room."

Penny tipped her head to one side, considering. Then she nodded. "Worth a try, anyway. It might create some buzz."

Branson threw his hands in the air, looking impatient. "You people are dreamers. Some Podunk carnival isn't going to raise the money you need, not in such a limited time frame."

"How limited?" Finn asked.

"The penalty will go up in two weeks. I don't think—"

"Do you have a better idea?" Penny asked him.

"Good fiscal management, maybe?" He stood up and grabbed his papers. "If you'll excuse me, I have some other responsibilities to attend to." He nodded at Kayla and Finn and walked out.

Kayla stared after him and then looked at Finn, one eyebrow raised.

"Don't ask me," he said. "Penny and Branson have some issues that go way back."

"Hello, I'm in the room," Penny said. "You don't have to talk about me like I'm not."

"Plus," Finn went on, ignoring her, "I think Branson takes care of his mother and a special-needs daughter. He's stretched pretty thin."

"He is, but that's not an excuse for shooting down every idea we have." Penny grabbed a chocolate-frosted doughnut and bit into it.

"What do you think of it all?" Finn asked her. "Because if you're in, then I think we should go full bore into this fund-raiser. But we shouldn't make the effort if it's all for nothing. You know more about the books than I do."

"I think it's worth a try," Penny said slowly. "But it would be an all-hands-on-deck sort of situation. That means you, Kayla. You brought up some great ideas. Are you willing to help?"

"Of course," Kayla said. "This place does important work. I would hate to see it go under. And the Lord knows I'm used to working against some odds." She did a half smile.

Finn's heart turned over. *Stick to business.* "I can cancel my weekend trip. This is more important."

Penny bit her lip. "I got a call this morning from my daughter."

"That's a surprise, right?"

Penny nodded. "She's been having some contractions. If it's labor—"

"Then you should go," Kayla said instantly. "We can handle things here."

"Yes," Finn agreed. "We can handle it." Penny never asked for anything for herself, always carried more than her share of the load. If she had the chance to mend things with her daughter—and be there when her first grandchild was born—Finn was all in favor.

"You guys are the best," Penny said. "It's probably Braxton Hicks. I should be able to stick around for a few days and help get this project going. And I can do the online fund-raising part from anywhere. It's just that there will be a lot of on-the-ground organization if we're really going to do an open house."

Finn blew out a sigh. Then he looked over at Kayla. "When should we get started?"

Penny and Kayla looked at each other. "No time like the present," Penny said. "Let's make a list."

Kayla grabbed a legal pad and a pen. "For starters, we need to think of what a good open house would be like. Something other people won't think of."

"That's true," Penny said. "We don't want to resort to carnival games and kettle corn. There's got to be something new that we could do to make people really want to come. If we're asking them to drive all the way up here, we ought to have something interesting and different for them."

"Something with the dogs?" Kayla said.

"Yes, but what?" Penny reached for the pad, but her phone buzzed and she glanced at it. Glanced again. Then she stood so abruptly that her chair tilted and would have fallen if Finn hadn't grabbed it.

"She went into labor," Penny said. "It's too early. I have to go."

"How can we help?" Kayla asked.

"I...I don't even know."

"Come on," Kayla said, taking the older woman's arm. "We'll get your things together."

So Kayla helped Penny pack while Finn called the airport, and within two hours he'd driven her there and gotten home again.

All the while, he was thinking.

He and Kayla were now pretty much committed to setting up an open house, and doing it alone. That was a problem, because every time he was near her he wanted to kiss her.

He had to get himself pulled together and realize, remember, what a bad idea that would be. For him, no; but for Kayla and Leo, most definitely. They'd already been through plenty of problems in their lives, and they didn't need him adding more.

For their sake, he had to keep control of his emotions.

The next morning, Kayla knelt in the meadow outside the kennels and watched Finn make his way up the road toward her, his gait unsteady. He was using his cane. It must be a bad day with his leg.

On impulse, she lifted her camera lens and started snapping pictures. With the morning sun glowing on the mountains behind him, the image was riveting. Something she could submit to a magazine or contest, if he gave her permission.

When he got closer she let the camera slip into her lap and surveyed the scene. Across the field, scarlet paintbrush flowers bristled toward the sky, while silvery lupine and blue columbine nodded and tossed in the faint breeze. Sage and pine sent their mingled fragrance down from the mountains. She'd brought Willie and Long John's dogs for the shoot, knowing they could be trusted to remain calm. Now Rockette lay at Kayla's side, big black head lifted to survey the scene. Duke, the grizzled pit bull, sniffed around the rocks, displaying a mild interest in a prairie dog that popped out of its burrow to look around.

Finn disappeared into the barn and came out a moment later, with Winter, the female who'd been abused, at his side. He approached Kayla with a half smile, half grimace. "Showing up as ordered."

"I'm sorry." She moved over to offer him a seat on the end of the bench. "You having a bad day?"

"It happens." He lowered himself onto the bench and propped his cane beside him. "What's our game plan?"

He sounded guarded, and she couldn't blame him. In fact, she was feeling the same way. They'd committed to a couple of weeks of working together on an important project, and that meant they'd have to deal with these undertones between them at some time.

If only they hadn't kissed. That had muddied waters that had only just started to clear as they'd adjusted to working together. Now she couldn't look at him without remembering his tenderness, wishing for it to happen again.

But getting close to Finn meant the risk that he'd discover their connection to the Airborne and that Mitch would find out. She couldn't let that happen, for her own safety but especially for Leo's.

Time to get businesslike. "I'd like to video you first."

His jaw literally dropped. "No way. This isn't about

me. I thought we were going to video Long John and Willie."

"Later. You first. You can talk about your work here, and about your history as a veteran."

"Nope. Not happening."

She blew out a breath, trying to keep her frustration under control. "We agreed yesterday that we'd make a series of short clips of veterans. Who better to start with than the person who pretty much runs this place?"

"*Willing* veterans. Which I'm not." He rubbed his leg and his face twisted again.

"If you're going to ask others to participate," she said, "you should be prepared to do the same. Tell your story. It will help other vets, and this place, and the dogs."

"My life isn't interesting!" He practically spit out the words and then lowered his voice. "It's a mess."

What was his story?

"Anyway," he grumbled, "I'm not exactly photogenic. I hate being on camera."

"You're inspiring," she said firmly. "And you can have the dogs with you. And we can edit it." She picked up the old video camera and panned the area, adjusting the settings. "Ready?"

He glared at her.

She glared right back.

He drew in a breath and let it out in a sigh. "Where do I stand?"

"Just sit right there." He was on a bench against the wood barn siding, Willie's dog, Duke, beside him, and if he wasn't photogenic she didn't know who was. He'd advertise the place better than anything. And he didn't even consider himself handsome, which was part of his appeal.

Now that he'd agreed, Kayla felt flustered. She was used to being behind a camera, but not to talking. "Let me find the questions I brainstormed," she said and went to her bag. *Be calm, be calm*, she told herself. *It's a job. You're just doing your job.*

And saving a ranch.

And making things right for Leo.

And helping dogs and veterans who need it.

She pulled out the sheet of notebook paper on which she'd jotted some questions and skimmed them over. They seemed kind of…shallow, and weak. She wanted to sparkle for Finn.

You're not a sparkling kind of person, said the voices from her past.

But it wasn't all about her.

She heard Finn's booming laugh and looked over. He was watching the two dogs. Rockette was rolling on her back in the grass, and Duke was poking and prodding her with his paw, letting out intermittent barks. Winter sat watching with mild interest.

She swung her camera around and caught footage of the dogs, then of Finn watching them. She walked closer.

"So, Finn, what do the dogs do for you?" she asked.

He looked more relaxed now, as he gestured toward the silly pair. "They're lighthearted, and always accepting, and they never give up. Old Duke here, he can't stop trying to dominate Rockette. And she won't let herself be dominated."

She quirked an eyebrow at him. "She's aware of the women's movement."

"She's her own dog, that's for sure."

"Could you tell us a little bit about the ranch and its mission?"

As he answered that softball question, he relaxed to his theme and was actually good on camera. His passion for the work showed, and he explained their clientele: vets who had lost hope, dogs who had lost their last chance.

She risked going a little more personal. "And what made you decide to work for the ranch? What is it in your background that makes you feel a connection?"

He frowned for a moment and then nodded. "I know what it is to lose hope," he said. "I served with good people. Some didn't come home, and some came home a lot worse off than I am."

When he came to a natural breaking point, she hazarded a more personal question. "Do you mind telling us about your own injury?"

"Do I have to?"

"Yes. Yes, you do." She put a hand on her hip, trying to look stern, and he laughed, and all of a sudden there was that romantic vibe between them again.

She cleared her throat and pulled herself back to a businesslike mind-set. "Seriously, if you don't mind, it will bring something personal to people."

"Okay." He looked off to the side as if collecting his thoughts, and then faced Kayla and the camera again. "I was caught in a building that had been bombed. A beam fell on me and…" He grimaced. "The fracture was too bad to fix just right."

She studied him. "What were you doing in the building?"

He shrugged. "Civilians were caught inside. One of my buddies, too."

"You went in to help get people out, didn't you?"
She knew in her heart that it had gone down that way.
Finn was a protector to the core. If he could help some-
one, he would.

"It needed done," he said. "We were able to get all the
kids out. This—" he gestured at his leg "—this didn't
happen until the last trip."

"Did you get a medal? Or probably more than one."
She thought of Mitch's stories of the actions that had
led to his medals.

Finn waved a hand. "Not important."

Maybe not, but she would look up his service record
when she got the chance, see what medals he'd earned,
or ask Penny. Because she was getting the feeling there
was a lot more to his service than he'd mentioned before.
And to have that in the video would add to its appeal.

Hearing about his heroism only made her more impressed with him. But she needed to remember her con-
cerns. "Could you tell us a little about your division?
Aren't the Airborne a tight unit?"

"Best in the army, at least according to us." He flashed
a grin. "We're definitely confident, but you have to be if
you're going to step out of a plane over enemy territory."

Kayla's stomach tightened. Of course he was proud
of his service and his brothers.

Of course, he was loyal to them. Just as Mitch was.

If they knew each other, they'd be loyal to each other.
So she simply had to make sure that never happened.

She heard voices in the kennel and quickly ended
the interview. She needed to be careful. She was getting so drawn to Finn. Just looking at him now, she
felt like it was hard to catch her breath. "Thank you,"
she said, feeling shy. "That was…well. I really admire

what you did, who you are." She felt like a dork, but she couldn't keep it in.

His face hardened. "Don't get too impressed. There's a lot about me that's far less admirable."

Willie and Long John came out through the kennel door, interrupting the awkward moment. "How'd they do as show dogs?" Willie asked, laughing as Duke jumped up on him.

"They were great. They could be pros." She pointed a stern finger at Long John, then at Willie. "Just so you know, I'll be interviewing you next, after the midday shift. And then we'll cut film into a good video we can use to promote our event."

"I'm ready, willing and able," Willie said, puffing out his chest.

"You're a ham." Long John waved a hand. "Now, me, I'd rather stay offscreen. I'm not the handsome dude I used to be."

Kayla smiled at the lanky man. "You're plenty handsome, and I'd guess the women, especially, will love to see you." She touched his arm. "And more important, your example of working through your issues will be inspiring. Both to donors and to vets who wouldn't otherwise think of coming."

"You're a good little lady," Long John said, his voice gruff. "We struck gold when we got you to come work at the ranch."

The praise warmed the hungry child inside Kayla. She put an arm around Long John's waist. "I feel like *I* struck gold, coming here."

"Yeah, sure, we're in the middle of a gold rush, but we also have to work," Willie said, gesturing back toward the kennel. "Those dogs won't exercise themselves."

"Of course!" Kayla hurried to put her camera away, determined to continue doing well at her regular job in addition to the extra she'd taken on.

"Kayla." Finn spoke quietly. "Why don't you take a break. We can handle the midday shift."

"Oh, no, it's okay. I'm glad to do it."

"Take a break." It wasn't just a suggestion.

He wanted her to leave. He was basically ordering her to leave.

Hot, embarrassing tears prickled the backs of her eyes and she swallowed. "Okay, then," she said. She gathered the rest of her things while the three men went back into the kennel.

She'd thought they had a connection. However reluctantly, Finn had let her in today, at least a little. Revealed something about who he was. She'd had a moment of thinking they were getting closer.

She dawdled on the road back to her cabin, trying to take in the mountains' beauty. Trying not to feel hurt at Finn's rejection.

She was starting to care what he thought, too much. And he was a dangerous man to care about.

But *was* he dangerous?

He didn't seem like the kind of man who would give her up to a fellow soldier. He seemed like he would want to protect her, take care of her.

On the other hand, she hadn't expected betrayal from the police officer she'd gone to when things went south with Mitch. She'd expected an officer of the law to protect her, and look how mistaken she'd been then. She had to remember where these men's loyalties lay.

Faced with an unexpected couple of hours to herself, Kayla walked inside her cabin. Grabbed a glass of iced tea from the fridge—and on impulse, her Bible and devotional book—and went back out onto the porch, Shoney trotting beside her.

She felt confused, like everything was shifting inside her, ready to explode. She didn't have anyone to talk to.

Except God.

She paged through the Bible restlessly, looking out over the fields and mountains. His world. So beautiful and perfect.

She knew He was in charge. You should trust Him. Moreover, there was nothing to do *but* trust Him, since her own power was so limited compared to His.

Her life hadn't been conducive to trusting. Not as a kid, not as an adult.

But God. God wasn't Mitch. God wasn't Finn. God was bigger, incomprehensible and great. He was like the mountains, mysterious, a little scary, and everlasting.

She let her eyes drift over the Psalms until they fell on a line in Psalm 92, one she'd underlined not long ago: *O Lord, how great are thy works! and thy thoughts are very deep.*

She breathed in and out and looked around.

She wasn't going to understand this world. She wasn't going to know what to do, not perfectly.

And no person was going to love away the bad things that had happened to her.

But God could, and would. According to the Book of Revelation, He would wipe away every tear.

She didn't know she was crying until a fat drop splattered on the parchment-thin page. She brushed her knuckles under her eyes and read on.

Read, and prayed, and listened.

Shoney seemed to sense her mood and pressed close

against Kayla's legs, and Kayla lifted the dog into her lap. Comfort and affection and unconditional love: God had known she and Leo needed those things, and had provided them through Shoney, whose special needs couldn't take away from her happy, giving spirit.

She nuzzled the dog's soft fur. *Okay, God. I get it. I should be more like Shoney.*

She kept reading and praying all afternoon. It was only when an alarm rang on her phone that she realized she'd have to hustle to go fetch Leo in time.

When she reached her car, she spotted Finn talking to Long John and Willie outside of Willie's cabin. The three men waved, and Willie gestured for her to join them.

She shook her head and mimed pointing at a watch. She got into the car and headed out.

There was a kind of peace in letting it all go, in realizing you weren't in control.

It was something she needed to keep exploring.

When her phone buzzed, she pulled over to take the call, figuring it was Long John asking her to run an errand while she was in town.

She didn't recognize the number. Maybe it was Willie's phone; he didn't use it often, so she'd never put him in her contacts.

"Hello?"

Silence at the other end.

"Hello? Willie?"

More silence. No, not complete silence. Breathing.

Horror snaked through her as she clicked the call off. She fumbled through the settings until she figured out a way to block the number.

She pulled in a breath and let it out slowly.

It was probably nothing. There was no reason to associate a random call with Mitch.

Anyway, once you'd blocked the number there was no way anyone could trace it. Right?

She put the car into Drive and continued on toward town, carefully, both hands on the steering wheel, staying a couple of miles under the speed limit.

She'd better not call attention to herself, lest the law enforcement here be just as corrupt as it had been back in Arkansas.

Chapter Eight

Almost two weeks later, Finn listened to the thunderous applause in the community center and smiled over at Kayla, who stood on the other side of the stage. She looked stunning in a white dress that fit her like a glove. Her brown hair fell loose and shiny around her shoulders, and her smile was as joyous as his.

They'd generated so much interest in the ranch, just by talking up the open house with friends and neighbors, that they'd been asked to share their story at the monthly town meeting. The event was tomorrow, and they'd been working like mad, but from the response they were getting, it seemed like it might actually be a success.

As the meeting broke up, people crowded around him, asking questions and offering congratulations. He looked over and saw a similar group surrounding Kayla.

Funny how conscious he was of her at every moment.

"Well, you done it," Long John said, clapping him on the shoulder. "I think you just got the open house a couple dozen more visitors. Folks are excited."

"That thermometer thing you put online is rising up

fast," Willie added, coming up behind Long John and reaching out to shake Finn's hand. In his other hand, he held up his phone, displaying a donation meter already half-full. He squinted over at Long John, then looked back at Finn. "Say, we need to talk to you a minute. In private, like."

"Sure." Finn glanced around, then ushered the two older men toward a quiet corner of the community center. "What's up?"

Long John and Willie glanced at each other. "We've got ourselves an awkward situation," Long John said. "See, we were given a gift card for that new restaurant up Cold Creek Mountain."

"Cold Creek Inn?" Finn whistled. "Nice."

"My daughter wanted to treat us," Willie explained. "Thinks I don't get out enough or some fool thing."

Finn chuckled. "Why don't you ask Dana Dylan to go with you?" He nodded at the white-haired dynamo who'd asked Willie out a number of times.

Willie raised his hands and took a step backward. "No, no way. I don't want to encourage her."

Finn lifted an eyebrow. "Because your heart's somewhere else?"

"His heart ought to go on out with Dana," Long John grumbled.

Finn shouldn't have opened that door. The two men's rivalry over Penny was mostly good-natured, but their friendship was too important to fool with them.

Apparently Willie felt the same way, because he slapped Long John's shoulder. "I'd rather have dinner with my buddy here than any woman. Don't have to clean up my act for him."

"Then you two use the gift card," Finn said. He was still confused about why they'd brought him into it.

"But we don't either of us like that kind of food," Long John said. "Nor a place where you have to get all gussied up to go."

"And it expires tomorrow," Willie said. "If my daughter finds out I didn't use it, she'll be upset."

"So we were thinking…"

"Since you and Kayla are all dressed up," Willie said, "I'd like for you to use it. Tonight." He held out a gilt-edged plastic card with *Cold Creek Inn* embossed in fancy script.

Mixed emotions roiled through Finn's chest. The thought of taking Kayla on a date sounded way too good. Working together as they had been, he was drawn to her more and more. She was a good person—that was the main thing. She tried hard and did the right thing and took care of her son. She said she wasn't a great Christian, that she had a lot to learn, but he'd watched her during church. She had a God-focused heart. The fact that she was gorgeous, at least to him, was just icing on the cake.

But the feelings Finn was having for Kayla were the exact reason he shouldn't be taking her on anything resembling a date. "I think you two should use it," he repeated. "It was meant for you, Willie, not me." And it would be better that way. Better than for him to start something with Kayla that he couldn't finish.

"I'm just not up to it today," Long John said. He gestured down at his body with a disparaging movement of his arm. "My Parkinson's is acting up. I need to get some rest."

"And I'm driving him back," Willie said. "Truth is,

I'm worn-out myself. I'd rather sit at home and watch reruns on the TV then go to some fancy place where I have to figure out what fork to use."

"Give it to somebody else, then," Finn said. He was starting to panic at the idea of doing something so romantic with Kayla. No telling where that would lead, but it was a place he couldn't go. "How about the Coopers. Isn't it their anniversary?"

"Nope," Long John said flatly. "Willie and I, we talked it over. We're giving it to you."

"Hey, Kayla," Willie called across the emptying room. "Come here a minute."

"Willie!" Finn scolded in a whisper.

But it was too late. She was already coming over, her high heels clicking, and again Finn was stunned at how gorgeous she was. "What's up?" she asked.

"Finn wants to ask you something," Long John said. "Come on, Willie. I see that old Pete Ramsey. He's always trying to borrow money. I need to get out of here." And the two men turned and walked away.

Although there were other people in the room—and in fact, Long John and Willie didn't go far before finding a couple of chairs—Finn suddenly felt like he was alone with Kayla.

If they went out to the restaurant, they would truly be alone. The thought created a tsunami of feeling inside him.

He tried desperately to cling to the thought that she might not be trustworthy, that there was some kind of mystery in her past. But he'd just talked to Raakib yesterday, and so far, there was nothing criminal or even dishonest to report.

"Finn?" Kayla was looking at him quizzically. "What's going on?"

She looked so pretty and sophisticated that he felt like a high school boy asking a girl to a dance. The ease he'd felt working with her was nowhere to be found. He held up the gift card. "Willie wants us to use this."

Behind her, Willie made a sweeping motion with his arm while shaking his head vigorously.

And the older man had a point. What a half-baked way to ask a woman out. "What I mean to say is, would you like to go out to dinner with me? At the Cold Creek Inn?"

Color rose in her face as she looked at him and bit her lip.

Oh, man. He *really* wanted to go out with her.

But did her hesitation mean she wanted to go, or that she didn't? He needed to give her an out. "You must be worried about Leo. You probably can't go."

"Actually," she said, holding up her phone, "I just found out he wants to stay a little bit longer at his friend's house. They're roasting marshmallows." She looked so pretty it made his heart hurt. "And his friend lives up Cold Creek Mountain."

"We do have something to celebrate," Finn said, with a smile and a tone he'd kept in cold storage for years. He stepped fractionally closer without even meaning to. "Today went well, and there's no one I'd like to spend the evening with more than you."

Her mouth opened halfway, and he couldn't take his eyes off her. He felt tongue-tied, until he again noticed wild gesturing behind her. Long John, and now Willie, seemed to be conducting a pantomime coaching session; Willie was making a rolling motion with his hands, as if to say, *talk to her more, convince her.*

So he started telling her about the restaurant, how fantastic it was reputed to be. "Apparently it looks out over the valley. They have all kinds of fancy game dishes, venison, and wild boar, and pheasant." But was eating wild game really persuasive to a woman? "I think they're known for their chocolate desserts, too," he said, hoping he'd remembered correctly.

"That sounds good." She gave him a tentative smile.

Finn noticed a couple of nearby people glancing their way. "Come over here," he said and guided her a little bit away from the crowd. "If someone heard us talking about the Cold Creek Inn, there goes your reputation."

"Because of going somewhere with you? Really?"

He thought. Not many people knew about what had happened in his past. And if they did know, would they see it as a reason for her to avoid him? He was starting to wonder. "It's a small town," he said, because he couldn't explain.

Although maybe, someday soon, he would. If anyone would look at his past mistakes with compassion, it was Kayla.

She shrugged. "I don't really care what anyone thinks. Do you?"

He didn't care about anything but her. "Nope," he said. "Let's get out of here." He offered her his arm, and she took it, and he felt like the most fortunate man in the world.

He glanced over his shoulder at Long John and Willie. They were both grinning and fist-bumping and thumbs-upping him. Because of course, they were trying to push him and Kayla together. Matchmaking. He should have realized it before.

He just hoped the two older men knew what they

were doing. Because Finn felt like he was diving into a sea of risks, and he couldn't predict the outcome.

When they walked into the Cold Creek Inn, Kayla's breath caught.

The dining room was full of well-dressed people, mostly couples. Waitstaff in white jackets hovered and smiled and carried trays high on one hand—a feat she'd only ever seen in movies. The decor was that of a hunting lodge, with rough-hewn wooden rafters overhead, a pine plank floor and wall hangings depicting hunting scenes.

But most impressive of all was the view. The whole front of the restaurant was glass, a floor-to-ceiling window, and it looked out over the valley. As the sun sank, pink and orange and gold filled the sky, and lights flickered on across the valley.

Breathtaking.

Kayla had read about places like this, had seen them on television, but she had never been. It was way out of her league, and a wave of anxiety washed over her. Would she know how to act, what silverware to use? Would she spill a glass of water or not know how to ask for the right food?

She was holding Finn's arm, his muscles strong beneath her fingers, and she must have tightened her grip because he looked down at her and patted her sleeve. "Pretty highfalutin for a couple of ranch hands," he said. "But let's just enjoy ourselves, okay?"

As the maître d' led them to a table by the window, she tried to walk with assurance. The man helped her into her seat while Finn took the chair across from hers and thanked him.

Even if she could handle this place, even if she didn't make a fool of herself, she still felt shaky about Finn. Had he really wanted to ask her out? Or was he just using up a gift card?

Regardless, he looked confident and sophisticated in his suit, his shoulders straining a bit at the fabric, his boots making him even taller than usual. Finn dressed up was just plain devastating. And she needed to pull herself together. She focused on the fact that it was a side of him that she hadn't seen before.

"Wait a minute," she said, pleased that she was able to sound light and casual. "I just realized I don't know much about your background before the ranch."

Some of the carefree light went out of his face. *Oh.* She hadn't meant to stir up the bad part of his past. "Did you live in LA or New York or something?" she added hastily. "Did you do client dinners at places like this?"

He laughed. "Far from it," he said. "My family's from Virginia. After the service, I got into agricultural sales. Fertilizer, seeds, stuff like that." He grinned. "At most, I'd take my clients to the town diner."

"But you seem so comfortable here."

He nodded. "My mom saw to it that we all knew not to slurp our soup or reach all the way across the table. Maybe once or twice a year, she'd grill us on our manners and then get Dad to take us to a fancy restaurant as a kind of test."

"That's so nice."

"I was fortunate," he said. "I had a great childhood."

She sensed he was about to ask her about her childhood, and that, she didn't want to talk about. "What does your dad do?" she asked, to forestall him.

"Small-town cop," he said. "Everybody loves him.

One of my brothers is a cop in the same department, and the other's a firefighter."

"Back in Virginia."

He nodded.

"Then...why do you live all the way out here?"

He looked out over the valley, now shadowed, with stars starting to appear above. "I'd been out here a few times for work," he said. "Liked the wide-open spaces. And when... Well, I needed a fresh start. Felt like I couldn't breathe, back East."

"I know what you mean," she said.

He looked at her sharply, but seemed to discern that she didn't want to talk about the negatives in her past. So he made her laugh mispronouncing various dishes, and joking about the particularly large trophy moose head that loomed on the wall behind her.

He was trying to make her feel comfortable, and she liked him even better for it.

Through the appetizers he ordered for them, the pheasant dish he recommended, the too-frequent refills of their water glasses by their overzealous waiter, he kept the conversation going. And Kayla was both pleased and dismayed to realize that she liked this side of Finn, too. She hadn't known he had a background that would lend itself to a place this classy, but it was nice to relax, knowing that he could handle everything.

"Dessert?" the waiter asked.

"Oh, I couldn't," Kayla said. She was full, and besides, they'd surely used up the gift card now. The prices on the menu had been scandalously high.

Finn looked at her with an assessing gaze. "Maybe we could take a look at the dessert tray."

"Of course, sir." And the waiter hurried away.

"Finn!" She laughed at him. "How are we going to eat dessert?"

A moment later, their waiter returned with a mouthwatering tray of cheesecakes, pastries, cakes and pies.

"That's how," Finn said.

She studied the treats. She'd never before experienced food that literally made her mouth water.

"Change your mind about being too full for dessert?" Finn asked, his voice teasing.

She smiled across the table at him. "Oh, yeah," she said. "I want that one." She pointed at a slice of chocolate cake that was layered with a raspberry filling, with extra chocolate sauce and whipped cream over the top of it.

"Good choice," Finn said. "I'll take the apple pie à la mode."

Of course they had to share their desserts. And of course their hands brushed as they did. Their tones grew lower as the sky outside turned black and candles were lit at each table. They seemed to be embedded in their own little world, a world of smiling and soft laughter and expressive glances miles away from their daily lives at the kennel and the ranch.

When she put down her fork, too full to eat anymore, Finn reached across the table and took her hand. "Kayla, I…" He trailed off.

"What?" One syllable was all she could get out. Even that was an effort, considering that she couldn't breathe.

He kept hold of her hand. "I don't know what's happening between us, but how would you feel about pursuing it?"

She looked at him and tried to remember all the reasons why she didn't want to. Tried to pull them back together into a coherent, reasoned set of ideas. But her doubts had scattered with the same wind that was making the moonlit pine branches below wave gently in the twilight.

It didn't seem like he would do anything to hurt her and Leo. It didn't seem like he would prioritize his military brothers over her. Could she trust him with her story? Was she strong enough to take care of herself and her child if things went south with Finn?

Most of all, could he really want to be with her?

Normally, in the past, she wouldn't have been able to believe it. The years of being unwanted were deeply embedded, so much that they seemed to always be a part of her.

But through her work at the ranch and the spiritual development she was gaining here, she was starting to have a different feeling about herself. A feeling that maybe, possibly, things might go well for her. People might want to be her friend. She might have found a place to belong.

Maybe Finn was a part of all that.

She looked at him and opened her mouth to try to put some of what she was feeling into words. But her phone buzzed with a text, and the waiter brought the check, and the moment was over.

Maybe it was just as well, but she couldn't help regretting it as she reluctantly pulled out her phone and studied the lock screen. "The marshmallow roast is over," she said to Finn. "Leo's ready to go home."

"Of course." He signed the check and stood. Came around the table to pull out her chair for her. "Let's go get him. It's late."

It *was* late. But Kayla's heart was full of promise as

they left the restaurant, Finn's hand barely resting on her lower back.

He was a good person, a person she could trust. A person who understood about Leo's needs, and maybe about hers, as well.

Maybe even a person she could build a future with.

After they'd picked up a very sleepy Leo and put him in the booster seat they'd transferred from Kayla's car earlier, Finn drove carefully down the winding mountain road.

A strange warmth surrounded his heart. He'd felt something a little similar with his wife, but way different in degree, like the difference between a candle and a roaring fire.

What he felt for Kayla was explosive, powerful, hot. He didn't want to go back to the friendly coworkers they'd been. He didn't want this night to end.

He heard Kayla murmuring over her shoulder, and Leo said something almost indistinguishable, and then Kayla spoke back.

"Music okay?" he asked, and when she nodded, he turned on the radio and found some quiet jazz.

It was always good to keep a kid calm right before bed. He remembered having arguments with Deirdre about that, when Derek was just Leo's age. Finn had liked to come home and play with Derek, but the excitement had meant the boy didn't want to go to sleep anytime soon. It had annoyed Deirdre, and now, from a more mature perspective, he could see why.

He'd been young, inconsiderate, all about his own desire to have fun with his son on his own terms.

If he had it to do over again...

He glanced over at Kayla. *Might* he have the chance to do it all over again?

He didn't want to be disloyal to Derek and Deirdre by having a good life when they'd been denied the chance. But his conversations with Pastor Carson over the past weeks had him thinking that maybe, just maybe, he didn't have to pay the price of his sin forever. Maybe the accident hadn't been entirely his fault. Maybe not even very much his fault, and though he'd always blame himself, at least to some degree, light and hope were slowly seeping back into his life. He was starting to live again. And Kayla was the reason why.

Thinking of the dinner they'd just had, he smiled. It wasn't the normal thing they would do together, wasn't something to be repeated often, but they'd made the most of it and they'd had a blast. He wanted that to be the case again, in other contexts. How would she like a rafting trip? A museum? A specialty food tasting? Marge's sled dog show?

He had the feeling that, with Kayla, anything would be fun.

"Leo's out," Kayla said and settled more deeply into her seat, facing forward. "He was exhausted. Thank you again for stopping to pick him up."

"I enjoyed it. I enjoyed the whole evening."

"So did I."

The words seemed to hang in the air between them, floating on soft notes of music. They hadn't gotten to discuss what he'd wanted to—whether she wanted to explore the connection they were feeling—but he'd read interest, at least, in her eyes.

He reached out and squeezed her hand, and the petite size of it in contrast to his own big paw, the mix of soft skin and tough calluses, moved him and made him want to explore her contrasts further.

They had a lot of ground to cover, a lot of background to reveal. He needed to tell her about what had happened with Derek and Deirdre. And he needed to know more about what had happened in her past, what had caused the bruises on her arms when she'd first arrived, what made her jumpy.

Needed her to know that he'd protect her from harm like that in the future.

He eased the truck through a narrow part of the road and came out onto a broad, flat stretch lit by moonlight. Pines loomed on either side of the road, casting shadows in the silvery light.

"It's beautiful," she said softly. "I've never been in a place so beautiful."

"I love Colorado. I wouldn't want to live anywhere else." Then he realized that sounded inflexible. "Though, I guess, for the right reasons—"

"No," she said, putting a hand on his arm. "You fit with this land, and that's a good thing. You're an important part of this community. You belong here."

She got that about him? He drew in a breath and thought he caught a whiff of the flowery scent of her hair. He wanted more than that, though; he wanted to bury his face in its softness, the softness she'd revealed tonight.

Be careful, some part of his mind warned his heart.

They were coming into a section of driveways and houses now, not exactly heavy population, but heavy for this area. Automatically, he slowed.

Suddenly, from a driveway, a car backed out in front of him. *Right* in front of him, going fast.

He slammed on the brake and veered left. He had to avoid the hit at any cost, because if they collided with another car...

Crash.

It was a slight crash, but it made a loud, metal-on-metal impact, and as the car rebounded back and started to rotate, he heard a scream behind him. Leo. Then it was joined by a higher-pitch female scream as the car hit a patch of loose gravel on the road and spun faster.

He kept steering into the spin, his instincts carrying him as his heart and mind freaked out.

It's happening again.

They're going to die.

It's your fault.

He pulled his mind out of that abyss and back into the present. He saw the cliff's edge coming at them fast, and with superhuman effort, he steered the car away. Time slowed down. They were just a few feet from the edge.

Inches.

Millimeters.

A hair's breadth from the drop-off, the car stopped.

Kayla unsnapped her seat belt and turned to the back seat, basically crawled right over. "Leo. Baby. Baby, it's okay."

She was speaking coherently, so that was one difference.

But Leo's sobs...

He couldn't look back to see what was happening to Leo. Had happened.

There was a knocking sound beside his head, but he couldn't turn to look at it.

He was somewhere else, in another car on another road at another time.

More knocking, then shouting. "Sir! Sir, are you all right?"

"Man, I'm so sorry… Oh, no, Dad, there's a kid in there." Some disassociated part of him heard the hysteria in the adolescent boy's tone.

There were noises. Someone opening the back car door. Voices: Kayla's. A stranger's.

In the distance, the sound of a siren.

His heart was still thudding hard in his chest. Sweat dripped down the middle of his back, soaked his palms that still clenched the steering wheel in a death grip.

With a giant sigh, he let his hands and his shoulders go loose. And then he couldn't hold himself up, or together, anymore.

Finn put his head down on the steering wheel and surrendered to the darkness.

Chapter Nine

The next morning, Kayla walked out onto her cabin's porch, coffee in hand, watching the sun break through a bank of clouds and cast its rays over the valley. Gratitude filled her heart.

They were okay. They were all okay.

Leo had a temporary cast on his wrist, and Kayla had a painful, colorful bruise across her shoulder and chest where the seat belt had dug in. She'd been terrified, of course, all through the ambulance ride to the hospital, until the doctors had reassured her that Leo had suffered no ill effects.

As for her resilient son, he'd loved the ambulance ride, the lights and the sirens. Future fireman or EMT, one of the guys had said, laughing as Leo begged to be allowed to sit up front and look at all the buttons and switches.

Finn seemed fine, physically, although he'd made himself scarce at the hospital, after a brusque question about whether she and Leo were all right. But that made sense. Delayed shock reaction, most likely. She couldn't wait to see him today, to talk to him about what had happened. During the car accident, but also beforehand, at the restaurant.

She wrapped her arms around herself, unable to restrain the big smile that spread across her face.

He liked her.

Finn, a real, honorable man, wanted to—how had he put it?—pursue a relationship. With her!

They had a lot to talk about. She was going to have to tell him the history with Mitch, let him know why she'd initially been so guarded. Now that she knew him better, she was pretty sure he would understand.

Behind her, she heard Leo call out, "Mom!" Footsteps pattered and then Shoney's tail thumped. She barked a happy greeting to her boy.

So the day was starting, Kayla would get Leo's breakfast and then help the ranch put on an amazing open house. There was so much to do, and she'd normally have been stressed out about it, but the events of last night had put it all in perspective.

She lifted her face to the sun's warmth and said a silent prayer of thanks: for their safety last night, and their freedom from Mitch, and for the fact that she and her son had found a home.

The day was a whirl of activity. They had almost double the number of visitors as they'd expected, due in part to their social-media sharing and in part to the word that had gotten out after the presentation last night. Everyone had to pitch in. Willie noticed that supplies of hot-dog buns and cola were running low, and took off in the truck to buy more. At the kennel tour, Long John talked up the dogs so positively that people started asking about adopting them. So Kayla set him up at a table with forms to handle that unexpected bit of new business.

Kayla led tours of the ranch, and Finn talked about the veterans' side of it. Penny, who'd just arrived back in town late last night, explained the organizational structure. They all pitched in to keep the free food and drinks coming.

The whole time, people kept coming up to Kayla and hugging her and telling her they'd heard about the accident, and were glad that she and Leo were safe.

When she got a free moment, she asked Missy how everyone knew about the accident.

"Small town," Missy explained. "And Hank Phillips kept telling everyone over and over about it."

She nodded. "He felt awful, and so did his son." The boy, backing out of the driveway on a new learner's permit, had stepped on the gas instead of the brakes, and the car had shot into the road right in front of them. He'd apologized over and over, and had barely managed to restrain tears. "The outcome could have been so much worse. I hope that poor kid doesn't stop driving forever."

"You're such a sweetheart, Kayla," Missy said, hugging her. "A lot of people would be angry. You're really generous, being so understanding."

Kayla waved away the praise, but she felt it. Felt like she and Missy might become friends.

Leo spent much of the day running around with his buddies from camp and church, making siren sounds and crashing into each other, reenacting the car accident. After a few efforts, she stopped trying to keep him still. Play was his way of processing what had happened, and even though he was fine, it had been a scary thing for all of them.

She hoped for an opportunity to talk with Finn about it, but every time she got a free moment, he was busy. And her own free moments were few, because in between tours, she was creating live videos and posting them.

When people finally started leaving, Penny beckoned her into the offices. "Check it out," she crowed, clicking into the crowdfunding page on the old desktop computer. She spread her hands, pointing them toward the full-to-the-top fund-raising meter. "Ta-da! We have enough to pay the back taxes and more!"

They hugged and did a little jig, taking it out into the driveway, where Leo and other kids saw and laughed and joined in. Then they all escorted the few remaining visitors toward the parking area.

Finally, Finn walked up to her and she started to open her arms. Everyone was hugging, right? But something in his face stopped her.

"Can we talk?" he asked.

"Um, sure." Some of her excitement seeped away as her inner danger alert sprang to attention. "We made a good amount fund-raising. Plenty to pay the taxes."

"Good. Let's walk." His voice was flat, his face without emotion.

She watched as he started away from her, leaning heavily on his cane. Something was different about him. His usual calm now covered over an intense energy.

"Did you get the response you hoped for from the veterans in the group?" she asked his departing back. Hurrying after him, she kept talking. "There were more of them than I expected. All different ages, too."

As soon as they were out of earshot of the others, he turned to her. "Look, it's not going to work between us."

She tilted her head to one side as her heart turned to a stone in her chest. "I don't understand."

He didn't look at her. "It's not complicated. I thought about it and I realized that this—" he waved his hand back and forth between the two of them, still without looking at her "—that this isn't what I want."

The old interior voices started talking. Of course, a man like Finn wouldn't want to be with a woman like her. It had been too much to expect.

But, she reminded herself, she *wasn't* that unwanted girl. She wasn't ugly. She wasn't bland and boring. People in Esperanza Springs liked her. People here at the ranch, too: Penny, and Long John, and Willie.

Finn still wasn't looking at her. Why wouldn't he meet her eyes? "Talk to me," she urged him. "Let's try to work it out, whatever happened."

He shook his head and looked off to the side. Like he didn't even want to see her face. "No."

Confusion bloomed inside. She couldn't understand what had caused him to erect this sudden wall, to refuse to share what he was feeling even though they'd been getting closer and closer these past weeks and especially last night. "Why are you being like this?"

"I'm telling you, it's not going to work."

She put her hands on her hips. "We have something, Finn! What we felt at the restaurant last night, what we've been feeling for a while now, it's worth exploring. You're a good man—"

He held up a hand like a stop sign. "It's *not* real."

"Did someone say something today? One of the visitors?" She couldn't imagine what might have been said, nor that Finn would be so sensitive about hearing it.

"No. The guests were fine." He drew himself up,

wincing slightly as he straightened his bad leg. "Look, you did a good job helping with the open house. We worked together, probably more than we should have, and it led us to think we had feelings for each other. That's to be expected."

Tears pressed at her eyelids as she tried to recognize the man she cared about in the squared jaw, the rigidly set shoulders. "Why are you doing this?" she choked out.

"Mr. Finn!" Leo came running up and stopped himself by crashing into Kayla, then bouncing off her to Finn. "Look at my cast!"

Finn closed his eyes for the briefest moment. "I don't want to look at it." He turned and started to walk away, his limp pronounced.

Leo ran a few steps after him. "But, Mr. Finn, I want you to sign it."

"No!" He thundered out the word.

Leo stared after him and then looked back at her, his face sorrowful. "Why is he mad at me, Mommy?"

Kayla sucked in her breath and tamped down the loss that threatened to drown her. "It's okay. Come here." She knelt and opened her arms, and Leo was enough of a little boy that he came running and buried his face in her shoulder. Her bruised, aching shoulder, but never mind. She clung to him fiercely.

Finn had seemed to be different from other men, but apparently, he wasn't. In the end he didn't care enough. The abrupt way he'd pulled back stabbed her like a dull knife to the chest. She might not have believed him, might have thought he was covering something up, except he'd been mean to Leo.

That wasn't the Finn she knew. But maybe she hadn't really known him at all.

She didn't understand it, but she was a person who accepted reality when it stared her in the face. She'd never believed in fairy tales, like some of the girls she'd known in school, imagining knight-like boyfriends who'd sweep them off their feet, visualizing wonderful, romantic wedding days.

But Finn was romantic and wonderful last night, a sad little voice cried from deep inside her heart. *He wanted to pursue a relationship. What happened to that?*

She shook off the weak, pathetic questions so she could focus on the real one: how to go on from here. Should she stay in the best community she'd ever known? The community where Leo had relaxed out of his hyper-vigilant ways and learned to be a kid again? The place where she'd started to feel at home for the first time in her life?

Could she stay, seeing Finn every day and knowing the brief flame of their relationship was doused for good?

Two days later, Finn still hadn't gotten over the awful feeling of rejecting Kayla and Leo. Pushing Leo away had been like kicking a puppy. Pushing Kayla away... that had just about ripped out his heart.

But that pain didn't even compare to what he'd felt when the car had spun out of control, when he'd heard Kayla's gasps and Leo's screams.

He'd spent the past two days driving himself hard, getting the kennels cleaned before Kayla got back from dropping Leo off at his camp. When she was around, he made himself scarce by painting a couple of rooms at the main house, mowing grass, even exercising the two horses.

His leg was so bad he couldn't walk without an obvious limp, but he couldn't stop moving. The shame of what he'd started to do—the way he'd almost put another family at risk—just kept eating at him.

Now, near sunset on Monday, he felt a mild panic. Two hours of daylight left and he was out of chores. His leg was throbbing, and he should rest it, but to stop moving would let the thoughts in.

He noticed the old shed behind the main house. They needed to pull it down, build something new on the slab.

He would do that now.

He got his chain saw and carried it around the shed, planning his work. It wasn't hard to see the symbolism: *you're real good at ripping things down, breaking things apart.*

And that's all you're good at.

He destroyed everything he touched.

The last person he wanted to see was Carson Blair, the pastor, but here he came in his truck, down from the direction of Kayla's cottage. Jealousy burned in Finn. Had she replaced him so quickly, so easily?

"Need some help?" Carson climbed out of his truck and Finn saw he was dressed in work boots and carrying a pair of gloves.

"No. I got this." He revved the chain saw.

"That's not what I heard." Carson crossed his arms and watched Finn as if he could see into his very soul. He probably could. Wasn't that in the job description of a pastor?

Finn started on the posts that held up the shed, taking satisfaction in the harsh vibration as he cut through them. Once he'd gotten through one side, he pushed at the shed with his foot.

"Hey, Finn!" It was Penny, calling from the back door of the main house. "I want some of that wood," she continued as she walked down toward Finn, the pastor and the shed. "It's weathered real nice. Got some things I could make out of it come winter."

"As a matter of fact, I know someone who'd like that door," Carson said. "Mind if I pull it off?"

Finn's intended task, a solitary demolition, was turning into a community event. Fine. He started pulling off some of the boards that were in good shape. "I'll get these cleaned up and bring them over," he said to Penny, hoping she would leave.

She didn't. "What's going on with you and Kayla?" She had her hands on her hips. Vertical lines stood between her brows.

"Nothing that needs to concern you."

"It does concern me," she said, "because they're thinking about leaving."

His head jerked around at that. He wanted to ask, *When? Why? Where will they go?* He wanted a way to patch the hole that her remark had torn in his heart.

But wouldn't it be best if they left?

"Finn," Penny said, "I like you. And I've put up with you and your darkness. The Good Lord knows we all have it. But the way you've treated her beats all." She grabbed a couple of boards and headed toward the house.

Finn glared after her. Maybe he'd been cruel, but it was kindly meant. Kayla and Leo would be better off without him.

He glanced over at the pastor. The man was removing the door from the shed, focused on the task, but Finn had a feeling he'd heard every word.

That impression was reinforced when the pastor spoke. "Anything you want to talk about?" He asked the question without looking at Finn.

"No." Finn walked over to his truck, started it and backed it up to the shed. He found a rope in the back. Tied one end to the truck hitch and the other to a side support of the shed. "Gonna pull it down. Watch out."

He put the truck into gear and gunned it a little, watching his rearview mirror. With a scraping, ripping sound, the shed tilted and then collapsed, boards jumping and bouncing before they settled, the metal roof clanking down.

It wasn't as satisfying as he'd expected it to be.

He stopped the truck, climbed out and limped over to the wreckage. His doctor was going to have his hide for working like this without a rest, messing up his leg worse than it already was. He tugged at the aluminum roof.

Without speaking, the pastor went to the other side and helped him lift the roof off and carry it out of the way.

"Thanks," Finn grunted.

"Why'd you hurt her like that?" Carson went back to the demolished shed and pulled out a couple of jagged pieces of brick.

"To not hurt her." Finn ripped at the corner of the shed that was still standing. The rough wood tore his hands. Good.

"What do you mean?" Carson tossed the bricks into a pile of debris.

"I was driving when my wife and son were killed!"

Carson didn't speak, and when Finn managed to look at his face, there was no judgment there. But, of course,

Carson was a pastor. He had to listen to all kinds of horror with a straight face.

Carson came over to help Finn tug at the stubborn corner post. "Does every person who's driving have total control over every circumstance on the road?"

Finn felt like he was choking. The pastor's words were bringing it all back, clear as if he were looking at a movie. He could hear his own voice, yelling at his wife. Her anger, the way she'd shoved at him.

He'd wanted to pull off the road. Why hadn't he pulled off the road?

Because it was a narrow mountain road. There was no place to pull off.

No place to escape the bobtail truck that had come barreling around the curve at a faster speed than it should have.

Just before impact, he'd caught a glimpse of the driver's face. He knew, now, that the driver hadn't died; that after being acquitted of any wrongdoing—although Finn seemed to remember something about a warning from the judge—the man had moved out of state.

The moments after the truck had rammed into them, he couldn't bear to relive. It was bad enough to have experienced the edge of it again when they'd had the near accident with Kayla and Leo.

"Well?" Carson gave the post a final tug and it came loose of its moorings with a scraping sound. He caught his balance and started tugging it toward the pile of debris. When he'd let it fall, he walked back toward Finn. "What do you say? Do you have total control?"

"No, but I should have." He tried to pick up a couple of loose boards, but his leg nearly gave out from under him. With a groan he couldn't restrain, he sat down on a stump. "I should have protected them." The lump in his throat wouldn't let him say more.

"I'm guessing you did the best you could at that moment." The pastor looked at him. "We aren't God."

Finn cleared his throat. "Why did God let that happen?" The words came out way too loud.

Carson looked at him steadily. "Talk to me about it."

"Me, Deirdre, that I can understand. We were fighting, and… But Derek was a kid. An innocent. He didn't deserve to die before he got to live!" Finn heard the anger and harshness in his voice. Anger felt better than raw grief, but not by much.

He hadn't known how angry he was at God until just this moment.

Carson wiped his forehead on the sleeve of his shirt and sat down on a pile of boards, a couple of yards away from Finn, not looking at him. Instead, he stared out toward the mountains. "I wish I had an easy answer, but I don't. Some things, we'll never know, not in this life. But your son is with Him, and I have to believe your wife is, too." He clipped off the words and looked away. "Some things we have to try to believe."

In the midst of his own raw feelings, Finn wondered about the pastor. He was a widower. How much had Carson worked through about his own wife's death?

Because he really couldn't stand on his leg anymore, Finn stayed where he was. He picked up a board, took the hammer from his belt and started pulling out nails.

Carson carried load after load of wood pieces over to the debris pile. When he almost had it cleaned up, he stopped right in front of Finn. "You don't have to suffer forever, you know. Maybe there was some sin in there on your part. There usually is. No one's perfect, but we *are* forgiven."

Forgiven. "Yeah, right."

"It's at the center of the Christian gospel. You know that."

A high-pitched sound came their way. It was laughter, Carson's girls. They ran toward the pastor, Leo right behind them. But when Leo saw Finn, he came to an abrupt stop. He looked at Finn a moment, both fear and reproach in his eyes.

Finn's throat closed up entirely. He busied himself with kneeling down—and man, did that hurt—to pick up some nails. Didn't want the kids to step on them.

"Daddy, come on! We caught a frog and a crawdad, and we wanted to keep them, but Miss Kayla said we better let them stay in the pond. But we took pictures, and Miss Kayla sent them to Miss Penny on her phone. Come see!"

A twin clinging to each leg, Carson looked over his shoulder at Finn. "Catch you later—maybe at the men's Bible study. We deal with some tough questions. Thursday nights." He lifted his hand in a salute-like movement and then followed his girls toward the car.

No way was Finn going to a men's Bible study. Bunch of brainiacs analyzing the deep hidden meaning of some verse of Scripture that no one cared about.

Although come to think of it…now that he was getting to know Carson, Finn realized it wasn't likely to be completely irrelevant.

It was only when he turned to head for his house that he noticed Leo was still standing where Carson's SUV had already pulled away. Looking directly at Finn. His face held sadness and longing and hunger. "Mr. Finn," he called.

That face and that voice made Finn want to run to the boy and scoop him up and hug him, tell him he *was* loved and that men—some of them, at least—could be protective father figures.

Except he wasn't one of those men.

With what felt like superhuman effort, he turned away from Leo and started walking toward his house.

A sound made him look back over his shoulder. Something like a sob. If Leo was crying...

"C'mere, buddy." Kayla knelt near Penny's place. Her voice sounded husky as she spread her arms wide.

Leo ran into them and she held him against her. Over the boy's shaking shoulder, she leveled a glare at Finn. And then her face twisted like she was about to cry herself.

Everything in him wanted to run to them, to hold them, to explain. To ask if they could try again, have another chance.

But that wouldn't be right, because for Finn, there couldn't be another chance. He couldn't *take* another chance.

He turned away and started walking.

It was the hardest thing he'd ever done. It felt like he was ripping his heart out of his chest and leaving it there on the ground, there with Kayla and Leo. But he was doing it for them, even though they didn't know it.

Kayla tried to brace herself for the task at hand. Straightened her spine and made herself move briskly, cleaning the dinner dishes off the table. It was now or never, though; she needed to pack tonight and leave early the next morning.

She drew in a deep breath. "Come sit by Mom, honey," she said to Leo. "We need to talk."

Leo had seemed dejected throughout dinner, and now, as he plodded over to where she was sitting on the couch, he looked resigned. Kids could sense trouble, and it was pretty obvious things had changed here at the ranch. Leo knew: something bad was going to happen.

It was only now she realized he hadn't looked like that in a while. Redemption Ranch had been good for him.

But no more.

"Honey," she said, putting an arm around him, "we have to move away."

She felt him flinch. He was so little to already understand what that meant.

He stared down at his knees. "Why?" His voice sounded whispery.

Because I can't stand being around Finn, loving him, not able to have him. Because I can't stand to see you get your heart broken over and over.

"We need to find a place where we can live full-time," she said. "This job was just for the summer."

"It's still the summer," he said in a very small voice.

"I know."

Was she doing the right thing? There was no question that tearing Leo out of this life would be hard on him. Staying would be hard, too. She was just trying to find the thing that would be the least painful for him. The way he had been getting attached to Finn, the constant rejection was hurting him. He needed to be around men who wouldn't reject him.

And Finn. The conversation she'd had with Penny had cinched her decision. "Don't judge him too harshly,"

Penny had said. "You and Leo remind him of his losses." She'd hesitated, then added, "His son was just Leo's age."

Penny's words had shaken her, put everything she knew about Finn into a different perspective. Even though she was furious at him for rejecting her and Leo, the deep shadows under his eyes spoke to her, tugged at her heartstrings.

If she and Leo caused Finn pain, it wasn't right for him to have to keep avoiding them. He had been here first. It was his place. He was the veteran. He was the one with the real skills.

"We're going to find another good place," she said to Leo.

"But I like this place," he said. "I like my friends."

"I know you do. You've gotten so good at making friends. You'll be able to make other ones." She tried to force confidence into her voice.

This was killing her.

He shrugged away from her and slid down to the floor. He lay down next to Shoney, who, as usual, was at their feet. The shaggy black dog rolled back into Leo, exposing her belly for a rub. "Shoney doesn't want to move." Leo rubbed the dog's belly and nuzzled her neck.

This was the worst part. "Shoney can't come."

"What do you mean?" Leo stared up at her, his eyes huge. Beside him, Shoney seemed to stare reproachfully, too.

"We're going to be driving a long time, and we'll stay overnight at some places that don't allow dogs." Kayla wasn't sure where they were going, but she'd found a couple of promising job possibilities online. "Once we find a new place to live, we'll have a lot of settling in to do. It wouldn't be fair to Shoney to take her to a brand-new place and leave her alone a lot, even if we were allowed to have a dog wherever we end up."

Kayla made herself watch as Leo started to understand. His eyes filled, brimmed over. She slid down to sit on the floor beside him.

"No, Mom!" Leo wrapped his arms around the dog, who obligingly nuzzled back into her son. "Shoney needed a home and we gave her one. We can't put her back in the kennel."

Kayla cleared her throat and swallowed hard. "We're going to take Shoney to Long John and Willie to look after."

"But Mr. Finn said they can't have another dog. He said it would be too much for them."

"Willie can keep her for a little while. Maybe after we get settled, we can get her back."

Leo buried his face in Shoney's fur. "We'll *never* get her back."

Kayla couldn't even make herself argue, because she knew it was probably true. And how sad that a little boy would have that realistic of an outlook, that he wouldn't be able to be comforted by kind platitudes.

She was kicking herself for letting them settle in this much. Why had she agreed to take Shoney? Of course Leo had gotten attached to her; they both had. But she should have thought ahead enough to know the job wasn't permanent.

To know things probably wouldn't work out, with the job or with Finn.

"I can help more." Leo sat up. "I can take her for more walks. I can feed her and clean up after her. You won't even know she's with us."

Kayla's heart felt like someone was squeezing it,

twisting, wringing. She shook her head. "You've been the best helper. But we still can't take her."

Leo buried his head in the dog's side and wailed.

Best to do this fast now. She stood and knelt beside him, rubbing circles on his back. "Do you want to come with me? Help me bring Shoney's stuff up to Willie's place?"

"No! No! I won't go!" He flung his arm to get her away from him, catching her cheekbone with his little fist. Pain spiraled out from the spot. That would be a bruise.

Leo's upset escalated almost instantly into a full-fledged tantrum, and she couldn't blame him. She felt like lying right down on the floor and kicking and screaming alongside him.

But she was the grown-up. Like a robot, she found her phone and called Penny over Leo's screams and sobs. "Can you come up and look after Leo for half an hour?"

"You're really going through with this."

"I have to, Penny."

Kayla loved the older woman for not arguing with her, for just saying, "I'm on my way."

By the time Penny arrived ten minutes later, Kayla had gathered all Shoney's things in a big box. Leo's crying had settled down into brokenhearted sobs, and he wouldn't let Kayla touch or comfort him. He just hung on to Shoney, who, bless her, allowed what amounted to pretty rough treatment without so much as a growl or nip.

"Have you tried to talk to him?" Penny asked, pulling Kayla into the kitchen area, where Leo couldn't hear them.

"He's too upset. He just keeps crying."

"I mean Finn," Penny said. "He's going around look-ing like someone shot his best friend. If the two of you could hash it all out, you might have a chance."

Kayla hated thinking of Finn being miserable. But he'd get over it, probably just as soon as she and Leo left the area. She shook her head. "The surprise was that he started to act like he liked me," she said. "He's an amaz-ing man. He could have any woman he wanted."

Penny dipped her chin and gave Kayla a pointed stare. "Doesn't seem like he wants just any woman. What if he wants you?"

"He doesn't. He told me." Kayla shook her head. "And anyway, that just doesn't happen for me."

"Kayla. You've got to work on—"

Kayla held up a hand. "I know. I'm a good person. Working here, getting away from…" She waved a hand in the general direction of the east. "From what was going on back in Arkansas, it's done so much for me. I appreciate your giving me a chance. I know you're the one who talked him into it in the first place."

"Do you know what happened with his wife and child?"

Kayla shook her head. "I don't need to know all that." She was curious, but knowing more details about Finn was likely to just add to her misery.

"You're making a mistake."

"Look, I've just got to take Shoney down to Willie's place before Leo and I both fall apart." She turned away from Penny, clenched her teeth together and walked over to Leo. "Come on, buddy. Let go of Shoney."

"No, Mommy. Please." He looked up at her, his face swollen and red. "Please."

She pressed her lips together to hold back the sobs and wrapped Leo in a hug. This time, his need for comfort overcame his anger and he collapsed into her arms, sobbing. They stayed that way for a couple of minutes. Shoney whined beside them and Kayla cried a little, too.

Be strong for him.

She drew in a gasping breath, then another. "Shoney will be okay. She'll miss us, but she'll be okay." She stood, staggering under Leo's weight as he clung to her.

Penny came over and reached out. "C'mere, buddy. We've got to let Mom go for a little bit."

Blinking hard against the tears, trying to breathe, Kayla took Shoney's leash off the hook by the door and attached it to the dog's collar. True to form, Shoney jumped and barked and tugged. She loved her walks.

Penny turned away, holding Leo tight. And Kayla walked an eager Shoney out the door.

At the bottom of Willie's porch steps, she knelt down and wrapped her arms around the shaggy black dog. "You've been a good dog," she said, rubbing Shoney's ears and the spots where her collar scratched her neck. Shoney collapsed down on her back, ecstatic with the attention, and Kayla tried to put all the love she felt into this last little bit of doggy affection.

The door of Willie's house opened and he came out onto the porch, backlit by the light from inside. Shoney sensed Willie's presence and jumped up, always ready for the next adventure.

Willie came down, rubbed the dog's head, and then picked up the box of Shoney's belongings and carried them up the steps.

Kayla buried her face in Shoney's coat, so soft and silky.

Shoney couldn't see, and she couldn't hear very well, but she made up for that in an ability to sense emotions. She licked Kayla's face and pressed closer into her arms.

Get it over with.

She picked up the dog, carried her up the porch steps and set her down, handing the end of her leash to Willie. "Thank you," she whispered.

Willie nodded, his weathered face kind. "I'll take care of her. She'll be all right."

Kayla nodded, turned and walked toward her cabin, her eyes almost too blurred to see. She couldn't go back and help Leo when she was a wreck herself. She stopped in the cool night air and drew in big breaths, trying to pull herself together.

Down at the main house, she saw a few lights. Penny had come in a hurry, leaving the place lit up.

And there was a single light on in Finn's place. The front room. She pictured him there in his recliner, reading. He liked old Westerns and Western history books. Rarely watched TV. They had that in common.

So, yeah, he was probably reading.

But she'd never know what.

The thought of that—that she'd never get to tell him a silly little thing like that she'd finished the Louis L'Amour book he'd lent her—made her shoulders cave in. The loss in her stomach and chest hurt too much. She wrapped her arms around herself.

She'd thought since they had all those weird things in common that they might have something. She'd imagined sharing books and listening to country music together, on into the future.

But it wasn't only about that.

It was about the caring in his eyes. The respect she

had for him as a man. The way they both worked hard at life, and tried to overcome past challenges with an upbeat attitude.

In the end, they *hadn't* overcome. She shouldn't be surprised, but she was. Like a fool, she'd gotten her hopes up.

She looked up at the stars and tried to pray, but God seemed as distant as they were.

She drew in a deep breath and let it out slowly. Then another. Good—she was steadier. She turned and marched toward her cabin.

Through the screen door, she heard Leo sobbing. Her heart gave another great twist.

"I don't know if I can do this, Father," she said to the cold, glittering stars.

But she had to. No choice, when you were a mom. She squared her shoulders and headed into the cabin.

Chapter Ten

The men's Bible study, which consisted of a circle of nine or ten men at Willie's house, was breaking up. Men stood, talked, helped Willie to clear away the refreshments he and Long John had made.

It was pretty obvious to Finn that Willie hadn't needed any extra help tonight. Calling Finn and saying he did had been a ruse, probably done in cahoots with the pastor.

Finn didn't really mind. Because one, he had nothing else to do; and two, he'd gotten thought-provoking ideas out of it.

Something bumped against his leg, and he looked down and saw Shoney. A bad feeling came over him. "What's she doing here?" he asked Willie.

"Kayla's leaving tomorrow, and she felt like she couldn't take Shoney along. She doesn't know where they'll land, what kind of place they'll live in or where they might have to stop along the way." He paused. "I put Rockette back in the kennel for now, but I can't leave her there."

That made him sigh, and he knelt and rubbed Shoney's sides, causing her to pant and smile.

She was okay now, with Willie. She was a resilient dog. But going back into the kennel, with her disabilities, wouldn't be a good thing.

And what must it have been like for Kayla and Leo to let Shoney go? They'd gotten so attached. Her blindness and deafness hadn't been any kind of barrier to them; they'd accepted her as she was, and they loved her.

It must have just about killed them to leave Shoney behind. The thought of it put a lump in Finn's throat.

The father of the boy who'd nearly hit their car came over and clapped Finn on the shoulder. "Glad to see you here tonight, because I wanted to thank you again," he said. "Without your driving chops, that accident could have gone a lot worse. If we had to collide with someone, I'm glad it was you."

Finn clenched his teeth to keep himself from snarling at the man. Finn wasn't glad it had been him, because it had broken him apart from Kayla and Leo.

But that was a good thing, right? Because it kept them safe. Safe from the unsafe Finn.

Who this man was saying was actually extra safe. That didn't compute at all.

"My son, man, he's still beating himself up about it," the man continued, oblivious to Finn's inner turmoil. "I wish he'd been here tonight to hear what the pastor had to say. We're none of us in control, not really, are we? Once something's past, you can't keep beating yourself up for it, I told him. You've got to move on."

"Right," he said as the man moved on to talk with someone else.

All the words he'd said swarmed in Finn's head and he didn't know how to process them.

We're none of us in control.

But he wanted to be in control. Wanted to be able to protect anyone on his watch.

He was the man of the family. He was supposed to be able to protect women and children. Back in the Middle East, his was one of the few units that hadn't had a failure in that regard. He hadn't killed any civilians, and neither had any of his men.

He supposed he'd come back cocky, thinking he was superhuman.

The punishment for that arrogance had come real fast.

He folded up the extra chairs and stacked them on the porch to carry down to the main house, then went back inside to see if Willie and Long John needed anything else.

They didn't, of course; they were fine. "Glad you could come," Long John said. "Mighty sad about that gal and her boy leaving us. Sure you can't talk 'em into staying?"

Long John's voice sounded plaintive, and Finn realized that these two old men had grown attached to Kayla and Leo, too. She'd listened to their stories, laughed at their jokes and appreciated their efforts to father her. And Leo had become a grandson to both of them.

"Sure am going to miss them," Willie said.

Everyone liked Kayla and Leo. No one wanted them to leave.

An idea of stopping at her place started to grow in the back of his head. She wasn't likely to forgive him for being so mean to her and Leo, but at least he could explain. Apologize. Pave the way for her to be able to come back for a visit, at least, see the old guys and Penny.

He hoisted the chairs to his shoulder, said goodbye to the last couple of men who were coming out of the cabin.

"Want me to drive those down the hill?" Bowie Briscol asked. "That's what I usually do when we meet here. No need for you to kill yourself hauling them."

Finn started to refuse and then thought, *Why not?* Obviously, Willie and Long John had manufactured the excuse to get him to come, but they'd had a good thought in doing so. They were doing their best to take care of him.

That was what Redemption Ranch was all about. People taking care of each other. And, he realized, he wanted Kayla and Leo to have the chance to be taken care of a little bit, too.

He couldn't repair the fragile thing he and Kayla had started to build, but could he maybe get her to agree to stay on? It had to be safer for her, better for Leo. They needed security and stability. Redemption Ranch could provide that.

He helped load the chairs into the back of Bowie's pickup, waved off the offer of a ride for himself and then strode toward Kayla's cabin, feeling more energized than he had since their falling-out.

There was a car outside Kayla's cabin. Not her old beater, but a late-model, city-style sedan.

Finn stopped and took a few steps back. Under veil of twilight, he watched as a tall, broad-shouldered man in a suit walked up to the door, opened it and went inside.

Heat rushed up Finn's neck. She'd gotten together with another guy this quickly? He'd been having all these *feelings* for her, and she was basically cheating on him?

Like Deirdre?

And with some suit in a fancy car, who probably had enough money to give her the life of luxury she didn't need, but probably wouldn't mind having?

His fists clenched and he hit the road to his place, making it home in record time.

When he got home, he went in the bedroom closet and started digging through boxes, frantic as a loon. He knew what he wanted to find and why.

It was a box of photographs of the years with Deirdre and, later, Derek. He'd hidden them away because it hurt too much to look at them, but he needed to now. Needed to remind himself what it felt like to live with a cheater. To remind himself that women couldn't be trusted.

He pulled out the wedding album, flipped through it and stuffed it back in the box. When those pictures were taken, they'd been happy, of course. Deirdre had been faithful to him, before the wedding and at least through the first year.

It was when he'd gone to the Middle East that she'd changed. He could track it in the pictures she'd sent, that he'd pasted up around his bunk like a fool, showed off to the other guys. She'd lost weight and done up her hair fancy, started wearing high heels.

She'd looked great.

Only when he'd come back had he realized she wasn't doing it for him—not for him alone, anyway.

They'd fought, separated, almost broken up, but then she'd gotten pregnant. It had infuriated her that he'd insisted on a paternity test, but given how much she was running around, it had only made sense to him. When Derek had turned out to be his baby for sure, he'd thought they could mend things between them.

And they had, for a while. The first couple of years of parenthood had been hard, but happy. But when Derek had entered his terrible twos, Deirdre had had her own rebellion.

She'd had issues, obviously. And Finn, young and immature and haughty, hadn't dealt with them well.

He shoved the photos back in the box and leaned against the bed, straightening out his leg, flexing it. The idea that he'd fallen for another cheater...

But even as he had the thought, he was comparing what he'd seen with the reality he knew.

Kayla wasn't the type who'd go into town and pick up some new guy in a bar, just because she'd had a fight with Finn. She just wasn't. And no, he and Kayla hadn't had a relationship, not really, but they'd had the beginnings of one. She'd felt it. She'd said it herself: *we have something here.*

And a woman like Kayla, feeling like that, wouldn't go looking for love somewhere else—not so soon, at least.

There had to be another explanation. A friend, cousin, brother. It would make sense if she'd called someone to help her out, and he should be glad she had a little male protection.

He didn't *feel* glad, but he knew he should.

As a matter of fact, he should call his detective friend and tell him there wasn't anything more to search for. Whatever secrets hid in her past, he didn't need to know them. Because through all that had happened, he'd actually learned to trust Kayla.

That was some kind of progress, at least.

He walked outside for some air, scrolling through his contacts to make the call, when the familiar, rattly sound of Kayla's car came along the road. It made him smile. He was always glad to hear it, glad she and Leo and that beater of a car had made it back to the ranch in one piece.

No sooner had he thought it than worry tugged at him. When she left the ranch, where would she go? Who would be there to notice she'd made it safely home? To worry if she hadn't?

He'd give her a call later, see if they could talk a little. In preparation for that, he lifted his hand in a wave.

She stared back but didn't wave in response. Her face was set, rigid. She gunned the bad motor and continued up the hill.

Well. Maybe talking to Kayla wouldn't quickly mend the broken bridges between them.

But at least he could call off his watchdog.

He found his friend's name and clicked the number.

Kayla drove the rest of the way up the dirt road that led to her cabin, confused. Why had Finn waved?

She was *not* going to get excited because the man had waved.

Leo, depressed about it being his last day of camp and about Shoney, had finally fallen asleep in the back seat. Fortunately, he hadn't seen Finn's semi-friendly expression. No use getting his hopes up again.

No use getting hers up, either.

Today had been her last day of work, too, and that had been hard; saying goodbye to all the dogs, working alongside Penny because Finn was AWOL.

Her heart was shredded and she had a million things to do and he *waved*?

She glanced back at Leo, his face sweet and relaxed

in sleep as it hadn't been since she'd let him know they were leaving. The day-camp group had given him a little goodbye party today, which was sweet. But not surprising. That was the way Esperanza Springs was.

She pulled up to the cabin and stopped the car. When she leaned into the back seat and tried to pull the still-sleeping Leo out, she could barely manage it. Asleep, he seemed to weigh a ton.

It had been so great when Finn had carried him to bed.

She shifted, getting her feet under her, getting him adjusted on her shoulder. She wouldn't have Finn helping her anymore. And guess what: she didn't need him. Her muscles were far stronger now than they'd been six weeks before, when she'd started at Redemption Ranch. And it wasn't only her muscles that were stronger. So was her mind and her confidence.

She shouldered open the front door. It was good to be home. Despite all the turmoil, she'd sleep well tonight.

She took another step and froze, just inches inside.

Why had the door been partly open? She always locked the door when she left.

Even as she reviewed the moments when she'd left the house, she stepped back. One step. Two.

The door swung the rest of the way open. And there, inside, stood Mitch.

She jerked back and Leo stirred, so she forced her body into stillness. How had Mitch found her? How had he gotten into her house? Where was his car? Sweat broke out on her face and back. "What are you doing here?" she asked around a stone of terror that seemed to have lodged in her throat. "Where's your car? How did you find us?"

"I pulled the car around back." He leaned against the

door frame and crossed his arms, and his presence in this place felt like a violation. "Oh, and by the way, that was a real cute photo of my son on one of the Eighty-second sites."

Kayla sucked in a breath. Had *Finn* posted a picture? Surely not, but…

"Nice how the name of the town was right there in the picture," Mitch said, his voice and stance casual, his eyes anything but. "Esperanza Springs Community Days. What kind of a town did you bring him to? It's not even American!"

"The Fourth of July." Kayla closed her eyes, just for a second. That soldier Leo had mistaken for Mitch. Kayla had gotten the man's wife to delete the photos with Leo, but several other people had been around. One of them must have taken a photo and posted it. Probably thinking a closed group website was safe.

No time to wonder why Mitch had been browsing through a random Eighty-second site. No time to wish she'd been more diligent about keeping cameras away from Leo.

They'd been found. Now she had to find a way to keep her son safe, against all odds.

Seeing Mitch brought back the last time, his big boots kicking her as she'd lain on the floor, trying to breathe, trying not to wake up Leo, gauging the distance to the door, escape, safety even as she'd known she could never leave her son in the house alone with his father, not even for a minute.

She backed to the edge of the porch. The worst thing she could do would be to go inside with him. Out here, with the stars starting to twinkle overhead and the cool, piney breeze from the mountains, she had freedom and a chance.

"Get in here." It wasn't a suggestion, but an order. "Want to talk to you."

Despite his casual posture, his hands were fists and his eyes burned beneath a furrowed forehead. If she ran for it, holding Leo, she'd only make it a few steps before Mitch caught them. Leo would wake up and be afraid.

If Mitch had to fight her and drag her inside, his rage would boil over. If she went inside as he'd asked, it might placate him for a moment.

She nodded and walked through the door and tried not to feel doomed when he closed it behind her. Despair and hopelessness wouldn't save her son. "Let me put Leo down."

Maybe Leo wouldn't have to see this and get traumatized again. Maybe she could talk Mitch down, make promises of seeing him tomorrow, get him to leave tonight. And then she could call Penny and Finn and the pastor and anyone else she could think of to get her out of this bind, because, yeah, she was independent, but she had people to help her now. She wasn't alone.

Mitch stood in front of her, blocking her way, and her stomach twisted. She'd forgotten how big he was. He could knock her out with one blow from his hamlike hand.

She knew. Knew, because he'd done it.

She straightened her spine. "Let me pass. I want to put him down so I can focus on you." *And get you out of here.*

His eyebrows drew together and he looked at her, suspicious, assessing. "Fine." He stepped to the side, not far. She had to walk within a couple of inches, close enough to smell his sweat. Her stomach heaved.

Keep it together. She'd thought to put Leo on his bed in the sleeping loft, but then he'd be a sitting duck, trapped. She didn't want him that far away from her. So she grabbed a blanket off the back of the couch, wrapped it around him and took him into the bathroom. She slid Leo onto the floor and put a towel under his head for a pillow. Thankfully he was a good sleeper.

She turned on the bathroom light, in case he woke up and was scared. *Please, God, whatever happens to me, protect him.*

Mitch stood in the doorway, emanating hostility she could feel like radiant heat. She turned, patting for her cell phone. Good—it was in her back pocket. She'd be able to get to it if he turned his back.

Which, from the hawk-like way he was watching her, didn't seem all that likely.

She walked right up to where he stood in the doorway, knowing that to show weakness would be fatal. "Come sit down," she said, feigning confidence and hospitality.

When he moved out of her way, she closed the bathroom door behind her. Anything to increase the chances that Leo would sleep through this, that he wouldn't get set back from all the progress he'd made.

"Would you like something to drink?" *Would you like to turn your back long enough for me to call for help?*

"Get me a beer," he ordered.

"Don't have any. Soda?"

He snorted in obvious disgust. "Fine." But he followed her to the refrigerator and stood too close, so she dispensed with the idea of a glass and handed him the can. Grabbed one for herself, too. It might come in handy. Lemon-lime carbonated beverage, square in the face, could sting, and a can could work as a missile, too.

She gestured him toward the sitting area and he plopped down on the couch. "Come sit by me."

Um, no. "I'll sit over here," she said, keeping her voice level as she felt for the stand-alone chair and sat down.

"Why are you acting so cold?" He banged his soda down on the end table.

Was he kidding? Hot anger surged inside her, washing away her fear. "You're an uninvited guest. You broke into my cabin. You expect me to roll out the red carpet?" And then she bit her lip. She had to stay calm in order to keep Mitch calm. It was tempting to scream out all the rage she felt at him, but she had to be wise as a serpent here, pretend a gentleness she didn't feel.

"You sure it's not to do with the big guy?"

"What big guy?" she asked, although she knew he must mean Finn.

How did he know about Finn?

"The one that lives right down the road and spends a lot of time with you," he said. "Finn Gallagher."

The surprise must have shown on her face, because he laughed, a high, nasty sound. "Oh, I've been watching you for days now. I know exactly what you've been doing."

She couldn't restrain a shudder. "What do you want with us?"

"You're my wife." His voice rose. "And he's my son. You left me. I have every right to bring you home."

She couldn't let this escalate. Something she'd read in a publication about dealing with aggressive dogs flashed into her mind. She relaxed her muscles and lowered her voice. "Mitch. I'm not your wife. We're divorced."

He glared. Apparently, what worked on dogs wasn't going to work on Mitch. And then his head tilted to one side as he shook it back and forth, and the whites of his eyes showed, and everything inside Kayla froze.

Mitch didn't look stable or sane. He barely looked human.

Every other time he'd been rough with her, he'd seemed angry—enraged, even—but he'd had his senses and he'd known exactly what he was doing.

His expression now made it seem like he'd lost it.

He stood and walked toward her, hands out. "I want you back."

"No, Mitch. Don't touch me."

He kept coming.

She jumped up and away from him and pointed at the door. "Go on. Get out of here or I'll call the police."

He seemed to get bigger, throwing back his head and shoulders and breathing hard. Heavy and threatening, he came at her.

She spun away. "I mean it. I have no problem calling 911."

"What're you going to call with, this?" He reached for the cell phone in her back pocket. She jerked away from his hand and heard her pocket rip.

He had the phone.

Miserable, hopeless thoughts from the past tried to push in: *You deserve whatever he does to you. This is the only kind of man who'll like you. No way can you escape him.*

But she was stronger now. Wasn't she? She *didn't* deserve Mitch's abuse. She wasn't alone; she had friends.

She'd even, for a little while, drawn the attention of a good man.

Finn respected her. Finn thought she was a good mother. A good person.

So did Long John and Willie and Penny.

She had to try to get Leo and run. Or maybe she could barricade them in the bathroom. She made a break for it, dodging Mitch, but he grabbed her arm and pulled it, hard. Pain ricocheted from her wrist to her shoulder, and she couldn't restrain a cry.

He took a pair of handcuffs—*handcuffs?*—out of his suit jacket and clicked one side to her wrist, the other to one of the wooden kitchen chairs, forcing her to sit. "Just in case you get any ideas," he said with a sadistic grin.

She tugged, but the cuffs held. And he'd cuffed the arm he'd hurt, so every effort shot pain from her wrist to her shoulder.

"Mommy?" The plaintive voice from the bathroom doorway made them both freeze. "Daddy!" There was an undertone of happiness there, but fear, too.

"Get back in the bathroom," Mitch snarled.

"But…"

"Go!"

Leo edged, instead, toward Kayla. She could see the sweat beaded on his upper lip, the vertical lines between his eyebrows, the shiny tears in his eyes.

"It's okay, honey," she said, trying to put reassurance into her voice and eyes, her free arm reaching for him without her being able to stop it. "It's going to be okay."

Leo took a step toward her and Mitch stepped between. "You pay attention to me, not her!"

He grabbed Leo's shoulder and walked him back into the bathroom, none too gently. Leo started to cry.

There was a swatting sound, and Leo cried harder.

She exploded out of her chair and headed toward the bathroom, dragging the chair behind her.

Mitch emerged, slamming the bathroom door behind him. From the other side, Leo sobbed.

"Stop right there!" Mitch dug in a black case against the wall and turned toward her with an automatic rifle in one hand and a hunting knife in the other.

Kayla froze, then sank back onto the chair. He'd truly gone over the edge. He'd always liked weapons, but he'd restricted their use to shooting ranges or country roads. He'd never pointed one at her, and he wasn't doing that now, but the threat was palpable. Not only to her, but to Leo, because a gun like that could make a wooden door into splinters in a matter of seconds.

A stray thought broke through her terror: not one of the vets she'd met at this ranch—Long John, Willie or Finn—would flaunt weapons so casually. Mitch wasn't a typical vet.

She looked around desperately, wondering how to escape or what to do, aware that if she made a wrong move, it might be her last.

On the counter was the big travel coffee mug Finn had given her when he'd noticed her rinsing and reusing a Styrofoam cup. He was a man of few words, but his actions said it all. He paid attention and tried to make her life a little easier, a little better.

She could trust him because of how he'd treated her. She should have told Finn the truth. Airborne or not, Finn would never have betrayed her to someone like her ex.

Mitch came closer and again she smelled his perspiration, tense and sour. He loomed over her. "You left me and took my son. You can't get away with that. You're going to pay."

He didn't care about Leo, had never been even an okay father, but she didn't dare to say it, not with him this volatile. She pressed her lips together.

Why had she made such a stupid mistake? Maybe if she'd been honest and up front with Finn, he wouldn't have dumped her.

Leo's cries were louder now, breaking her heart. "Let me go to him," she pleaded. "Just let me talk to him a minute."

Mitch turned toward the bathroom. "Shut up!" he thundered.

But Leo's crying only got louder.

A desperate plan formed in her head, and without a moment's hesitation, she put it into action. "Give him my phone," she said. "He likes to play games on it. He'll quiet right down." And maybe, God willing, he'd use his five-year-old technology skills to call for help. She'd taught him how to use the phone to call 911, and he knew how to call Penny, too.

Mitch hesitated. Leo's wails broke her heart, but they obviously grated on Mitch. He pulled her phone out of his pocket and headed toward the bathroom.

Please, God.

He hesitated at the door and looked back. She tried not to betray anything on her face.

"You're trying to get him to call for help!" He kicked the bathroom door. "You shut up in there, kid, or I'll hurt Mommy."

Leo's cries got quieter. From his gulps and nose-blowing, it was obvious he was trying to stop.

Poor kid. If they could get out of this alive…

Mitch came back over and squatted in front of her. "Suppose you tell me what you thought you were going to gain from leaving Arkansas." He glared at her. "Go on—talk. This ought to be good."

Discouragement pressed down on Kayla.

"Talk!" he yelled, shaking the leg of the chair so that she nearly fell off.

From somewhere inside her, outrage formed and grew. There had been a time when she'd thought she deserved bad treatment, that it was the best she was going to get, but she knew differently now. "I left because I wanted a fresh start for me and Leo," she said, chin up, glaring at him. "I refuse to live a life hiding from you and terrorized by you."

Mitch looked…startled? Was that worry on his face? She'd never stood up to him before.

"You unlock these handcuffs and go back where you came from," she ordered, sweat dripping down her back.

He raised a hand. He was going to punch her.

"Don't. You. Dare." She put every bit of courage and confidence she had into the words.

Mitch stepped back and looked around. "What was that?"

"What?" Was he seriously going to pretend he'd heard something to avoid a confrontation with her? Hope swelled. "You didn't hear anything. Unlock these cuffs!"

"I heard something." He lowered his weapon and moved to the window of the cabin like a cop in a TV movie. A bad movie.

If she could just get to her phone, which he'd left sitting on the chair…

She tried to scoot, quietly, while he leaped around the room, pointing his weapon into every corner. She got within a yard of the phone. If she could move a few inches closer…

"Aha!" he yelled as he leveled the rifle at her.

And Kayla realized two things.

No matter how weak Mitch ultimately turned out to be, he was holding a deadly weapon.

And he *really* didn't act a bit like the veterans she'd gotten to know over the past two months. "Were you ever even in the Eighty-second Airborne?" she blurted out before she could think better of it.

He roared something indistinguishable and came at her.

Chapter Eleven

Finn had been wrestling with God, and God was winning.

Guilt about his past mistakes with his wife, he was realizing, had made him into a worse person. Maybe that was why God forgave mistakes. Because to spend time punishing yourself for all your past sins meant you weren't much good to anybody in the present moment.

Further, he realized that he did want to be involved with people. He wanted to be a husband and father again and do it right this time.

He'd never entirely get over what had happened with Deirdre and Derek. He'd always wonder whether he might have been able to save their lives if only his reflexes had been faster, his speed lower, his focus more intent.

But he wanted to go on living. And that had a lot to do with Kayla and Leo.

His phone buzzed, and he was relieved to escape his own thoughts. He clicked onto the call. "About time you called me back," he said to his friend.

"I have very little to report," Raakib said. "Believe me,

my friend, I tried, but I haven't found anything against Kayla. From all accounts, though, her ex-husband, Mitch, is bad news. Quite volatile."

It was nothing more than what he'd expected. He knew Kayla was good. Even without someone vouching for her, he knew it.

Crunching gravel outside the window marked Penny's arrival at her place. Unlike Kayla's car, Penny's had a quiet, well-maintained sound.

Kayla's car. Worry edged into his awareness.

When Finn had been getting jealous of the man in the suit, Kayla hadn't even been in her cabin. So what was the guy doing there? "What does her ex look like?" he asked Raakib.

"Sharp dresser," Raakib said. "Tall, about six-two. Large, because apparently he's obsessed with lifting weights. Though not as large as—"

"Gotta go," Finn said. "I think he's here."

He clicked off the call and grabbed his gun and ran outside. Penny was getting out of her car with a load of groceries.

"Drive me up to Kayla's," he barked. "I think her ex might be here."

Penny's face hardened. She dropped the bags and got back into the car. Finn got into the passenger side, and she gunned the gas the moment he was in.

The car he'd seen before was gone. But Kayla's was there.

So maybe it had just been a friend of hers, who'd visited and left, and Finn would be making an idiot of himself. But he wasn't going to take that risk. Not with Kayla and Leo.

"Whoa—wait," Penny said as she pulled in beside Kayla. "Look at that."

Finn looked in the direction she was pointing. Willie was coming up the road at a pace that was almost a run. Behind him, Long John limped as fast as Finn had ever seen him go, Leo beside him, holding his hand.

It would have looked comical, except for the intent, angry, scared expressions on all three faces.

And the fact that both Long John and Willie had weapons at the ready.

Finn had to salute their courage, but mostly, he had to get to Kayla before they did. "Keep them back," he said to Penny and ran to the cabin door.

Finn walked in on chaos. The man in the suit was on the ground, on top of Kayla. But Kayla was scrambling out from under him. A chair fell and knocked into the man—Kayla almost seemed to be jerking the chair around—and she punctuated that blow with a kick in the man's face.

She might even be winning the fight, but Finn couldn't wait for that to happen, especially with the automatic weapon on the floor near the man.

The man was going for it.

No.

No way. Finn moved faster than he ever had in his life, leaping onto the man just as his arm reached for the weapon.

The man was strong, burly. He landed a good punch on Finn's face.

"Get the weapon," Finn yelled, and Kayla rolled and stretched her arm and grabbed it.

The door banged open just as Finn started to get the

jerk under control. "Sorry," Penny called, "I couldn't hold them back. Leo, wait!"

"Mom!" Leo ran to Kayla.

Finn got the guy into a full nelson. He saw that Penny had secured the gun. Kayla was laughing and crying, one arm wrapped around Leo. "How did you get out?"

Leo puffed out his chest and grinned.

"Kid climbed out the bathroom window," Willie said, shaking his head in obvious admiration. "Came running down and got us."

Finn's prisoner—who had to be Mitch, Kayla's ex—started to struggle.

"I could use a hand here," Finn said, breathing hard. "We need to tie him up."

"I've got some handcuffs," Kayla called, "if you can take them off me and get them onto him."

Only then did Finn realize that Kayla had been fighting this fight while handcuffed to a wooden chair.

Her hair was coming out of its braid, her face red and scratched, the sleeve of her shirt ripped. He had never seen anyone so beautiful.

"Key to the handcuffs," Penny barked at the man, who stopped struggling and actually looked a little cowed. He nodded toward his side pocket.

"I'd get it," Penny said, "but I don't think I can stand to touch him."

Willie extracted the key from the man's pocket, none too gently. Penny freed Kayla and handed the key back to Willie and Long John along with the handcuffs. A moment later Mitch was sitting in the chair, his hands cuffed behind him.

"Those military pins you're wearing," Long John said. "What unit were you in?"

"Eighty-second Airborne," he mumbled.

Finn's head jerked around at that. "Seriously? Dates of service?" This guy did *not* seem like any paratrooper Finn had ever met. More like one of the wannabes that sometimes hung around veterans' events acting way too aggressive and boastful. "I think we're gonna check on that."

"What's your full name?" Long John, who prided himself on keeping up with the latest technology, had his phone out and was clicking on it.

"It's Mitchell Raymond White," Kayla said.

"Friend in veterans affairs owes me a favor," Willie said. "Think I'll give him a call."

"Where were you stationed?" Finn asked. "And I didn't hear you say your dates of service."

Mitch looked away. "I was on special assignment."

Right. Finn looked over at Kayla and Leo. Kayla met his eyes, her own wide and concerned. But Leo was talking excitedly, explaining how he had climbed out the bathroom window.

Good. The boy wasn't listening. He didn't need to learn about his father's deception this way.

Willie clicked off his phone. "They never heard of him."

"He's not in this record, either," Long John said, scrolling through his phone's screen.

Finn glared at the lowlife cuffed in the chair. "Stolen valor is a pretty serious offense."

"Especially when you've been getting veterans benefits for years," Kayla said from the corner, her voice indignant.

Willie drew himself up to his full height—about five-five—and glowered at Mitch. "Between that crime and what you tried to do to this woman and child, young man, you're going to be behind bars for a good long time."

Penny fussed over Kayla while Willie called the police and Long John tended to some scratches Leo had gotten jumping out the bathroom window.

As for Finn, he sat off to the side, against the wall, his mind reeling.

Something terrible had almost happened, and together, they'd managed to stop it. Kayla and Leo were safe. And he made a decision: he wasn't going to waste another moment.

Whatever Kayla felt, he knew his own heart.

But when he turned and really studied her, he noticed she was holding her arm tight to her side. "Do we need an ambulance?" he asked Penny, who was kneeling beside Kayla, running her hand over her shoulder, arm and wrist.

"Not for me," Kayla answered promptly.

"Maybe a quick visit to the ER or the Urgent Care," Penny said. "I don't think your arm is broken, but it's definitely sprained. Here, let it loose."

As Penny held Kayla's arm straight to examine it more carefully, Leo watched with a little too much concern in his eyes. "Hey, Leo," Finn called softly, and the boy looked his way. "You did a real good job today."

A smile tugged at Leo's mouth. And then he ran and jumped into Finn's open arms.

Finn's heart swelled almost to bursting as he held the wiggly little boy, then put him down to hear, again, the story of how Leo had screwed up his courage and climbed out through the window to find help for his mom.

Leo was hungry for praise; well, Finn was glad to

give it to him, because what he'd done had been more than praiseworthy.

Finn had a hungry heart, too, and talking to the little boy, commending his quick thinking and agility, seemed to fill it up a little.

He and Leo might be good for each other, he reflected. And as he distracted Leo from the distressing sight of his father being led away in handcuffs, as he talked about ways Leo could help his mom while her arm healed, he felt like he'd been given a second chance.

If only he could convince Kayla to take a chance with him.

A week later, Kayla strolled the midway of the county fair, with Leo holding her hand and Finn beside her.

She wondered what to do.

Rather than packing up the car and moving away, she and Leo had stayed around, at first to give evidence against Mitch, and then to let her arm heal a bit, and now...

Now it was decision time. Tomorrow would be the back-to-school information day. All the kids at Leo's camp were talking about it—the start of first grade was a big deal—and Leo wanted to know: Would he go to school here, or were they moving somewhere else?

She didn't know the answer.

They'd fallen back into their routine here. Leo had been attending camp. Kayla had helped with the dogs as best she could, given her wrenched arm. Shoney had come back, first for a visit, and then an overnight to sleep in Leo's bed, and now somehow she was back to living with them again, her old accepting, ecstatic self.

Finn had been friendly and helpful, but a little guarded.

They hadn't really had the chance to talk in depth, because Leo, understandably, was sticking pretty close to Kayla's side.

Mitch had gone to jail, then gone before the judge, and then somehow managed to post bail. With no contacts in Colorado, and forbidden to see Kayla or Leo, he'd gotten permission from the court to go back to his job in Arkansas. Kayla suspected he would also try to destroy evidence of his fraudulent claims of military service, but the likelihood was that he'd be charged with a federal crime. That was because he'd received benefits and discounts he wasn't entitled to.

She still worried about him, and would until he was behind bars. But with Finn, Penny, Long John and Willie on high alert—and friends back in Arkansas reassuring her daily that Mitch was there, going about his routines—she found she was able to relax.

She wouldn't go back there, but she might move on. She liked mountain living, but there were plenty of places, especially here in the West, where she could have it.

The problem was, Finn wouldn't be there.

Penny had talked to her about taking on some additional duties as they worked to expand the ranch. They'd need cleaning and cooking help if they were to open the old bunkhouse.

Everything in Kayla longed to stay in this community where she'd made friends and felt valued, where Leo was happy and social, where the mountains loomed good-heartedly over the flat bowl of the valley, reminding her on a daily basis to look up to God.

But if staying meant watching Finn move on, take up with other women, become a distant friend, she didn't know if she could bear it.

Too much thinking. She squeezed Leo's hand and inhaled the fragrances of cotton candy and fry bread.

"Mom! There's Skye and Sunny!" Leo tugged at her hand. "Can I go see them, please?"

"I'll come with you," she said and then looked questioningly at Finn. "Want to come along?" They'd basically ended up together at the fair by accident, and she didn't want to assume he intended to stay with her and Leo.

But he smiled amiably. "Whatever you two want," he said and followed along.

That was how he'd been acting. Like he wanted to do things with her and Leo; like he cared. But there was a slight distance. They hadn't talked about why he'd pushed her away before, and it kept a wall between them.

"Leo!" Skye called as they approached. "We're going to go do the pony rides. Can you come?" She clapped a hand over her mouth and looked up at her father. "Oops. I'm s'posed to ask first. Daddy, can Leo come with us?"

Carson fist-bumped her. "Good job remembering, kiddo. And of course Leo can come."

"Can I, Mom?"

Not can *we* go, but can *I* go. He was growing in independence and she was glad and sad all at the same time.

"I'll watch over him," Carson said. "It's run by folks in our church and it's supersafe."

"Sure," she said, and instantly the three children ran toward the other side of the fairgrounds, Carson jogging after them, calling for them to wait.

That left her and Finn, standing together. It felt awkward to Kayla, so she looked out across the valley. The sun was low in the sky, just starting to paint the tips of the mountains red. God's reminder that He lingered with them, even in the dark of night.

"Do you want to ride the Ferris wheel?" Finn asked abruptly. "Over there," he added, gesturing toward the little midway.

How did she respond to that? *Yes, I want to do that because it seems incredibly romantic*? *No, because I don't want to get closer right before we go away*?

"Scared?" he asked, his eyes twinkling down at her. "I'll hold your hand."

That sent a shiver through her. She wanted him to hold her hand, not just now but into the future. He was looking at her funny, and she almost wondered whether he was having the same thought.

But then, as they headed toward it, he kept looking at his watch. Was he bored? Eager to get back to the ranch?

"The line's kind of long," she said, giving him an out in case.

"That'll give us the chance to talk."

Oh. He wanted to talk. Kayla tried to ignore the tremor in her core.

As soon as they got in line, he turned away from the loud family group in front of them. "Why didn't you tell me about Mitch?" he asked quietly.

She looked up at him. "I asked myself the same question, when I thought he'd got us trapped for good. I...I should have. But Airborne Rangers are so loyal, and I'd bought into his story."

Finn's mouth twisted. "Beneath contempt. All of it."

"I know. I still can't believe he maintained that lie for so long. And I feel like a fool for buying into it."

"You had no way of knowing." He shook his head. "Those guys...they're good at concealing what they're doing. He'll pay for it. But, Kayla." He put his hands on her shoulders. "Even if he *had* been a military brother, I would never choose someone else over you."

Kayla's throat tightened and she felt the tears glitter as she looked up into Finn's eyes. He was being sweet; he was being kind.

But she couldn't quite trust his kindness. "Why'd you push me and Leo away, Finn? That really hurt."

He nodded, studying her face. "Do you have some time?"

A half smile tugged at the corner of her mouth. "The line's moving pretty slow." The group ahead of them was playing a guessing game now, Mom and Dad obviously trying to keep their young kids occupied. Behind them, a pair of teenagers stood twined together, clearly focused only on each other.

Finn drew in a deep, slow breath. "You know my family died in a car accident."

She nodded.

"Well, I…I was driving."

"Oh, Finn." She stared at his troubled eyes as the implications of that sank in.

No wonder he was so mired in it—tortured, even. How would you recover from something like that? She took his hands and squeezed them. "I'm so sorry. How awful that must've been."

He nodded. "I was officially exonerated, but…" He shook his head slowly, meeting her eyes briefly, then looking away. "I've lived ashamed for a long time."

His dark sadness, the way he drove himself, all of it made more sense now. Of course Finn would beat himself up, even over an accident that wasn't his fault. He was a protector to the core, and to not be able to protect his family, to have been driving when they were killed… Wow. She put an arm around his waist and squeezed, because she couldn't find anything sufficient to say.

"Next!" The attendant barked out the words.

Finn helped Kayla climb into the narrow-seated cart, and then turned back and spoke to the attendant in a low voice. The attendant looked at him, looked at Kayla and then shook his head.

Finn moved and reached for his wallet. She couldn't see what he was doing. Paying the attendant? They hadn't gotten tickets, but she'd thought rides came with the price of admission.

"Let's get a move on," somebody yelled from the line, the voice good-natured.

Finn climbed into the seat beside her and fastened the bar over them, carefully testing it for security.

"Were you giving that guy a hard time?" Kayla asked.

Color climbed Finn's neck. "You could say that."

As the Ferris wheel slowly filled up, and their car climbed incrementally higher, Kayla looked out over the fair, the town and the broad plain, sparkling with a few lights from far-flung homes and ranches. Her heart gave a painful squeeze.

She loved this place. She loved the land and the people and the discoveries she'd made here, the strength she'd found.

The trouble was, she loved Finn, too. And to stay here loving him… Well, that would be hard and painful. Not just for her, but for Leo, who had also come to care for the big, quiet soldier.

Most likely she *couldn't* stay, but that made her reckless. "Tell me about the accident," she said. "What happened?"

He took a breath and looked around as the Ferris wheel jolted them to the next level. "You really want to know?"

Something told her that for him to tell it was important, was maybe a key to his healing. If she couldn't be with him, she could at least do that much for him. Be a true friend. She reached for his hand and squeezed it. "I want to know."

He looked down at their interlaced hands. "So I was driving, and we were having a fight. What it was about doesn't matter now."

She nodded, sensing that he needed to tell it his own way, at his own pace. The twilight, the small passenger car, the separation from the noise of the fair, made it seem as if they were alone in the world.

"She took Derek out of his car seat."

"While you were driving?" She stared at him. "What mother would do that?"

"She wanted to get out, wanted me to stop. But it wasn't safe, because there was no shoulder to the road. So I kept driving. I was yelling at her to buckle him in again, to fasten her own seat belt, but instead, she grabbed the steering wheel and jerked it."

"And that's what..." She looked at his square, set jaw, the way he stared unseeingly out across the plain, and knew he was reliving what must've been the worst moment of his life.

He cleared his throat. "We went straight into a semi-truck bobtail."

"And they were both killed." She said the last word steadily, because she sensed that it all needed to come out into the open.

"Instantly." He hesitated, then met her eyes. "I was buckled in. I came out of it with barely a scratch."

"Wow." She'd been holding his hand through the whole recitation, but now she brought her other hand around to grip it, to hold his hand in both of hers. "That must have been so, so awful."

"I wished I had died. So many times. What kind of a man lets his family be killed while he walks around healthy and whole?"

She hesitated, looking up at his face. Around them, the noise and lights seemed to dim. "I don't want to speak ill of someone I don't know, someone who's dead, but it does sound like she caused the accident."

He nodded. "That's what the police report concluded, and I know that in my head. In fact, I'm still angry at her for taking Derek out of his car seat. If he had been buckled in, most likely…" He looked away, his throat working.

"Yeah." She remembered how she'd felt when Mitch had upset Leo, how she'd worried that the hurting would become physical. That was really what had prompted her to leave. But to have a partner actually cause your child's death… Her own throat tightened, and she cleared it. "Nothing I can say can make that better, but I am so sorry."

"It doesn't make you hate me?" He sounded like he really thought she might.

"Of course not!" To see this big, experienced soldier look so insecure, so torn apart… All she could do was put both arms around him. Not as a romantic thing, but for comfort. Friend comfort. It was a short hug, and then she let him go so she could meet his eyes. "If we were blamed for all the awful things that happened to us, nobody would escape unscathed. Look, I know I'm not to blame for being abused by Mitch. At the same time, I made a bad choice in marrying him. Maybe you made some bad choices, too." She reached up and ran a finger along his square jaw, feeling the roughness of his whiskers. "You're human, Finn. Just like everyone else."

He closed his eyes, nodded slowly and then looked at her. "I've started to make my peace with it."

"The men's Bible study?"

"That, and the pastor, and some thinking and reading I've been doing."

"I'm working on making my peace about Mitch, too." Finn would understand that. He would know that resolving such big issues in your past didn't happen all at once. It was a process, one that would never be fully completed, not in this world.

She'd barely noticed that the Ferris wheel had filled up and that they were moving fast now. But as they went over the top and sank down, her stomach dropped and quivered. She wasn't sure if it was the Ferris wheel or the company, but she squeezed Finn's hand and giggled when it happened again.

He put an arm around her. "You *are* scared," he said. "Chicken!"

"I'm not!" she said with mock indignation. "Look at this." She lifted her arms high in the air.

"Whoa!" He grasped her hands and put them back firmly on the bar in front of them. "Don't do that to me."

So she put her head on his shoulder as the ride continued, then slowed and finished. The cars jerked as people exited the Ferris wheel, but when it was their turn, the operator skipped past them.

"Hey, you missed us," she called back to him, but he didn't seem to be listening.

Oh, well. She didn't mind being here with Finn for a little longer. She looked up at him and noticed beads of sweat on his upper lip. Was *he* the one afraid of the Ferris wheel? Somehow, with his life experiences, she didn't think so.

Now they were back at the top of the Ferris wheel, and it creaked to a stop. She leaned over the edge and looked down. The whole wheel was empty except for them. "Hey," she yelled down. "You forgot us!"

"Kayla."

She jerked around to look at Finn, because there was something strange in his voice.

"Kayla," he said quietly as he took her hand, lifted it to his lips and kissed it. "Kayla, I'm no good at this, but I…I…"

She cocked her head to one side, staring at him. "What? Finn, what is it?"

"It's not a spot to get down on one knee, and anyway, I can't do that too well, not with my bad leg. But…" He reached into his pocket and pulled out a small box. Opened it and then looked into her eyes. "Kayla, I don't want you and Leo to leave. I want you to stay, and not just stay as a coworker. I know it's fast, and I know a lot has been happening in your and Leo's life, but…"

Kayla couldn't breathe.

"So I know it might take you a little time, but for me, I'm more sure about this than I've ever been about anything in my life. I love you, Kayla. I want to marry you. I want to make a family with you and Leo. And if you say yes—even if you say you'll consider it—I promise to protect you and care for you for the rest of my life."

It was more words than she had heard from Finn, all at once, since she'd met him. Warmth, even a banked fire, shone in his eyes. He was holding her hands so gently.

She felt tongue-tied.

"At least look at the ring?"

"Oh!" She looked down and saw a simple square diamond on a white gold band. She reached out and touched it with one finger, and the sharp hardness of it made her realize that this wasn't a dream, that this was real. The most real thing she'd ever experienced, and the best.

And yes, she should wait and think and make sure. But no way. "Nothing would make me happier than to marry you. And Leo, well, I know he'd be completely thrilled to have you as a dad."

He clasped her to him and held her, and the swelling emotion in her chest made her dizzy. "I want to be a dad to him," he said. "But if he needs to stay in touch with Mitch, I understand that and I will help to make that happen."

Her heart melted at his words. She suspected that Finn could be jealous and possessive, but he was willing to work with Mitch to make things good for Leo. That was selflessness.

He touched her chin, and when she looked up at him, his face was framed by stars. "Did you really say yes?"

She smiled. "Yes! Yes, I said yes!"

He let out a quiet exclamation and lowered his lips to hers.

As he kissed her with a restrained intensity that warmed her all the way to her toes, she felt like her shoulders were loosening, her chest was opening, and she was free. Free of that feeling of being unwanted. Free of having other people think she was a mistake.

He lifted his head and smiled at her. From the ground, she heard the sound of cheering.

"Do people know what you're doing?" Suddenly it all came together for her. "Did you plan this? Did you tell the attendant?"

A sheepish expression came onto his face. "I'm sorry, but I did have to get a few people involved. Carson knows. That's why he brought the twins by, to help get Leo out of the way."

From below, she heard a shout. "Mom! Did you say yes?"

"Leo knows?"

Finn rolled his eyes and shook his head. "He wasn't supposed to. But I guess Carson let it slip to the girls. That or the ride attendant or the jeweler spilled the news. It's a small town." Then he leaned over the edge of the cart and waved. "Hey, Leo. She said yes. That okay with you?"

Kayla might have been the only one who heard the uncertainty in his voice.

"Yes! Yay!" Leo cheered, and others were talking and laughing and cheering, too. The Ferris wheel slowly rotated their car to the ground and stopped, and there were all the people she cared about: Penny, and Long John and Willie, and Carson and the twins. And of course, Leo. When the attendant opened the bar, Leo ran to them. She opened her arms, and Finn opened his, and Leo leaped into them.

"Want to go for a quick spin as a family?" the ride attendant asked, his eyes crinkling at the corners.

"Yeah!" Leo yelled.

And as they both hugged him, then tucked him carefully in between them, talking and laughing—and in Kayla's case, crying—the warmth and rightness of it overwhelmed her. She looked up at the sky, and the stars seemed a canvas on which God had written His plan. "Thank You," she murmured. "Oh, Father God, thank You."

Epilogue

Four months later

Finn stood at the front of the little church, and even though his fancy tie was half choking him, he couldn't be happier.

"I can't stand weddings," Finn's veterinarian friend Jack DeMoise said from his position behind Finn.

"That's no way to talk, young man," Willie said. It had been a toss-up for Finn which of the two older men should be his best man, but Long John had insisted he didn't want the honor; he had other plans for the wedding. Plans, as it turned out, to walk Kayla down the aisle.

So it was Willie and Jack who stood up with Finn, and Carson who was doing the ceremony. Finn knew what it was to have a band of brothers, but this group wasn't bonded just by fighting; they were bonded by life. They were family.

The changes that being with Kayla and Leo were already working in him felt like a gift from God. He'd been closed in, hurting, before, such that joy couldn't gain a foothold. Now he felt joy every day.

Kayla, too, was changing and growing. She and Leo had been seeing a counselor, trying to deal with Mitch and what he'd done. Both of them seemed to stand taller, as if burdens they'd been carrying had been lifted from their shoulders.

The music changed, and he looked down the church's short aisle. There was Leo, a cute little man in a suit and new cowboy boots, standing straight and serious with his responsibility of carrying the rings. He walked forward slowly, biting his lip, and then he looked up at Finn. Finn gave him an encouraging nod and smile, and Leo started to speed up. Soon, he was running full speed, clutching the satin ring pillow in his fist.

What could Finn do but kneel down and open his arms to the little boy who already seemed like his own son?

He got Leo straightened out and standing in the right place, and looked up in time to see Penny, already halfway down the aisle. Her dress was simple, her hair loose, and behind him, he heard Willie suck in a breath.

Poor Willie. If only everyone in the world could be as happy as Finn was.

Next came Kayla's friend Janice from back in Arkansas. She'd come for the wedding and basically fallen in love with the place, and Finn wouldn't be surprised if she moved out here sometime soon.

And then he lost focus on everything else because there was Kayla. Her classic wedding dress, sleeveless and ivory and fitted, looked incredible. Rather than a veil, she wore a wreath of flowers.

She had a lightness in her steps, a lift to her face that was completely different from when she had arrived at

Redemption Ranch. She was radiant, and it wasn't just a figure of speech. She glowed.

She held Long John's arm and Finn wasn't sure who was supporting whom, but they both looked happy.

Kayla caught his eye as she got closer, and love shone out from her eyes, as deep blue as a Colorado sky. This time, he was the one who sucked in a breath.

"You're a blessed man," Carson said, and Finn looked sharply at him.

"It's the simple truth," Jack said from behind him. "You know me and Carson wish you all the happiness in the world." There was a hunger in his voice. Neither Carson nor Jack thought they could have this kind of happiness. They had talked about it a lot in the men's Bible study.

Of course, a year ago, Finn would have never guessed he could have this kind of happiness, either.

As the music swelled, Long John delivered Kayla to Finn. He was taking his fatherly role seriously. "You better be good to this woman," he said to Finn, his voice stern.

"I intend to." Finn watched as Long John sat down and then centered his full attention to Kayla.

Kayla, soon to be his wife.

His heart soared as the pastor began the simple ceremony. Against all his expectations, he'd been given a second chance. With a woman so well suited that they seemed to have been made for each other.

They had both had their share of grief and tribulation. But maybe that just made this happy time all the sweeter.

"I love you," he said to his bride, keeping his voice low.

But not low enough. "You're getting ahead of yourself," Carson said, and the congregation laughed.

"I'm okay with that," Kayla said. "I love him, too."

"Then can we be done and go have cake?" Leo asked.

"Just a few minutes, buddy," Finn said, rubbing Leo's hair.

So Carson made quick work of the ceremony. And then came the cake and congratulations, toasts and dancing. It felt good to be surrounded by their friends, old and new.

But after a couple of hours, Finn pulled Kayla aside. "You had enough of all this?" he asked.

She nodded up at him, her eyes shining. "I can't wait until we're alone together."

He put a hand on either side of her face, leaned down and kissed her lightly. "We're the bride and groom, so we don't have to wait," he said. "What do you say we take off?"

Her eyebrows shot up. "Can we?" she asked. "Without saying goodbye?"

"We have to go through the hall to do it. Should we try?"

Of course, they didn't make it, because Carson and Jack had their eyes open for just such a move. While Finn and Kayla found Leo and said goodbye to him—he was staying with Penny, but had plans for daily visits with Carson and the twins—the news that they were leaving spread through the crowd.

When they made a run for the borrowed old Cadillac they were taking to their brief mountain honeymoon, they were pelted with birdseed. And sometime while the reception had been going on, the car had been decorated with signs, tin cans and shaving cream.

But that was all fitting, because they were starting their lives together as part of a community. A nosy, interfering community, but one that wanted the best for every member, where neighbors were quick to extend a hand.

Once in the car, Finn leaned over and gave Kayla the thorough kiss he'd been longing to give all evening, earning catcalls and cheers. He looked into her eyes. "Are you ready?" he asked.

She nodded, her eyes locked with his. "I'm so ready," she said. "Let's go."

* * * * *

If you enjoyed this story, try these books in
Lee Tobin McClain's RESCUE RIVER *miniseries:*

ENGAGED TO THE SINGLE MOM
HIS SECRET CHILD
SMALL-TOWN NANNY
THE SOLDIER AND THE SINGLE MOM
THE SOLDIER'S SECRET CHILD
A FAMILY FOR EASTER

Available now from Love Inspired!

Find more great reads at www.LoveInspired.com

Dear Reader,

Thank you for visiting Redemption Ranch! I'm very excited about this brand-new series, where troubled veterans and abandoned senior dogs heal together... and where romance has the wide-open space to grow. Finn, Kayla and young Leo have plenty of challenges to overcome, but with God's help they learn to love one another, becoming the happy family God intended them to be.

One reason I love writing Christian romance is that I can delve into big problematic issues. That's partly because the pages that *aren't* taken up by love scenes can be devoted to character development. But mostly, it's because the difficult problems people face can be best solved by turning to God. Faith and faith communities are the healing forces that let Christian romances dive deep, and still come back for an uplifting, happy ending.

May your summer be filled with faith, love and good books,

Lee

Get 4 FREE REWARDS!

We'll send you 2 FREE Books plus 2 FREE Mystery Gifts.

Love Inspired® books feature contemporary inspirational romances with Christian characters facing the challenges of life and love.

FREE Value Over $20

YES! Please send me 2 FREE Love Inspired® Romance novels and my 2 FREE mystery gifts (gifts are worth about $10 retail). After receiving them, if I don't wish to receive any more books, I can return the shipping statement marked "cancel." If I don't cancel, I will receive 6 brand-new novels every month and be billed just $5.24 for the regular-print edition or $5.74 each for the larger-print edition in the U.S., or $5.74 each for the regular-print edition or $6.24 each for the larger-print edition in Canada. That's a savings of at least 13% off the cover price. It's quite a bargain! Shipping and handling is just 50¢ per book in the U.S. and 75¢ per book in Canada*. I understand that accepting the 2 free books and gifts places me under no obligation to buy anything. I can always return a shipment and cancel at any time. The free books and gifts are mine to keep no matter what I decide.

Choose one: ☐ **Love Inspired® Romance**
Regular-Print
(105/305 IDN GMY4)

☐ **Love Inspired® Romance**
Larger-Print
(122/322 IDN GMY4)

Name (please print)

Address   Apt. #

City   State/Province   Zip/Postal Code

He knocked, and stood there staring when a young, beautiful
woman opened the door. Chestnut-colored hair peeked out
from her *kapp.* It matched her warm brown eyes and the
sprinkling of freckles on her cheeks.

There was something familiar about her. He nearly
smacked himself on the forehead. Of course she looked
familiar, though it had been years since he'd seen her.

"Hannah? Hannah Beiler?"

"Hannah King." She quickly scanned him head to toe.
She frowned and said, "I'm Hannah King."

"But…isn't this the Beiler home?"

"*Ya.* Wait. Aren't you Jacob? Jacob Schrock?"

He nearly laughed.

"The same, and I'm looking for the Beiler place."

"*Ya,* this is my parents' home, but why are you here?"

"To work." He stared down at the work order as if he
could make sense of seeing the first girl he'd ever kissed
standing on the doorstep of the place he was supposed to
be working.

"I don't understand," he said.

"Neither do I. Who are you looking for?"

"Alton Beiler."

LIEXP0718

"But that's my father. Why—"

At that point Mr. Beiler joined them. "You're at the right house, Jacob. Please, come inside."

He'd never have guessed when he put on his suspenders that morning that he would be seeing Hannah Beiler before the sun was properly up. The same Hannah Beiler he had once kissed behind the playground.

Alton Beiler ushered Jacob into the kitchen.

"Claire, maybe you remember Jacob Schrock. Apparently he took our Hannah on a buggy ride once."

Jacob heard them, but his attention was on the young boy sitting at the table. He sat in a regular kitchen chair, which was slightly higher than the wheelchair parked behind him.

The boy cocked his head to the side, as if trying to puzzle through what he saw of Jacob. Then he said, *"Gudemariye."*

"And to you," Jacob replied.

"Who are you?" he asked.

"I'm Jacob. What's your name?"

"Matthew. This is Mamm, and that's Mammi and Daddi. We're a family now." Matthew grinned.

Hannah glanced at him and blushed.

"It's really nice to meet you, Matthew. I'm going to be working here for a few days."

"Working on what?"

Jacob glanced at Alton, who nodded once. "I'm going to build you a playhouse."

Don't miss
A Widow's Hope by Vannetta Chapman,
available August 2018 wherever
Love Inspired® books and ebooks are sold.

www.LoveInspired.com

LIEXP0718

Looking for inspiration in tales
of hope, faith and heartfelt romance?

Check out **Love Inspired**® and
Love Inspired® **Suspense** books!

New books available every month!

CONNECT WITH US AT:

Ignoring the tilt and rumble of the HH-60G Pave Hawk
helicopter about to hoist her down below, Senior Airman
Ava Esposito adjusted the sturdy harness sleeves around
the black nylon sling holding the sixty-five-pound yellow
Lab that was about to rappel with her. Roscoe's trusting
eyes followed her while he hovered close to her chest.

"That's right. It's showtime. We've got to find that little
boy."

Roscoe wouldn't understand, but they were armed and
ready for anything or anyone they might confront in the
dense woods that belonged to Canyon Air Force Base.
This reserve covered hundreds of acres and could hide
a person for weeks if not months. Right now, she had to
find a lost little boy and watch her back for a serial killer
who'd escaped from prison in the spring and was reported
to be back in these woods.

Her focus humming on high alert, Ava checked her weapons and equipment one more time. Then she patted the alert K-9 on his furry head. "Ready?"

Roscoe woofed his reply.

Nodding, she scooted to the open side of the chopper and let her booted feet dangle out, Roscoe's warm breath hitting the inch or so of skin she had showing outside of her heavy camo uniform, protective combat vest, knapsack and M16 rifle.

Above her, a crew member adjusted the carabiner holding the pulleys that would hoist both Ava and Roscoe so they could rappel down, each with their own pulley to hold them securely together.

Nothing but heavy woods, scattered rocks and hills. But somewhere out there was a lost, scared little boy.

Something whizzed past her. But even with the chopper's bellowing roar all around her, she heard the ding of metal hitting metal.

And then she saw it. The ricochet of a bullet hitting the fuselage. Someone was shooting at them!

Love Inspired®

Inspirational Romance to Warm Your Heart and Soul

Join our social communities to connect with other readers who share your love!

Sign up for the Love Inspired newsletter at **www.LoveInspired.com** to be the first to find out about upcoming titles, special promotions and exclusive content.

CONNECT WITH US AT:

Harlequin.com/Community

 Facebook.com/LoveInspiredBooks

Twitter.com/LoveInspiredBks

LISOCIAL2017